Theo is becoming convinced that Clothilde Trahan brings nothing but trouble to his life.

"That doesn't look safe, sir."

Theo jammed the hammer into his belt and cast a glance over his shoulder. She'd almost closed the distance between them, and she strolled along with a basket hanging from her elbow. The sight of her caused his mouth to go dry. If he didn't find her so irritating, he just might find her. . .what?

Attractive? Noonday sun glinted off blue-black hair that hung in a thick braid reaching nearly to her waist. Yes, he did find her quite pretty.

So what?

Pretty girls were a dime a dozen. He'd seen his share and would most likely see a good number more before Jesus called him home. Canada probably had a whole slew of them just waiting for his arrival.

So what if a girl in yellow caught his eye?

He'd be gone in no time, and she'd just be a memory. Whether she was to be a good memory or a bad one remained to be seen.

Clothilde Trahan stood at the bottom of the ladder now, and he had to lean down to see her face. "How about I do my job and you go do yours, whatever that may be, eh?"

"I *am* doing my job." She shaded her eyes and squinted up at him. "I'm going to be the teacher here, and this will be my school. As such, I felt I should come see how you were getting along."

"Your uncle and the pastor agreed to this? To you being the new teacher, that is."

She dropped her hand and looked away. "They will."

Theo chuckled. "That's what I thought. You're no more the teacher here than I am."

KATHLEEN MILLER Y'BARBO is an award-winning novelist and sixth-generation Texan. After completing a degree in marketing at Texas A&M University, she spent the next decade and a half raising children (four) and living in such diverse places as Lafayette, Louisiana; Port Neches, Texas; and Jakarta, Indonesia. She now lives with her nearly grown brood near Houston, Texas, where she is active in Fellowship of the Woodlands Church as well as being a member of American Christian Fiction Writers, Romance Writers of America, Writers Information Network, and the Authors Guild. She also speaks on the craft of writing at the elementary and secondary levels.

BOOKS BY KATHLEEN MILLER Y'BARBO

HEARTSONG PRESENTS
HP474—You Can't Buy Love
HP529—Major League Dad
HP571—Bayou Fever

Don't miss out on any of our super romances. Write to us at the following address for information on our newest releases and club information.

Heartsong Presents Readers' Service
PO Box 721
Uhrichsville, OH 44683

Or visit www.heartsongpresents.com

Bayou
Beginnings

Kathleen Miller Y'Barbo

Heartsong Presents

To Mimi. I know you would have loved a houseful of little ones just like Mama. Well, maybe not *exactly* like Mama. . .

To Dana. Research diva and real live Trahan. You are such a special gift from God. *Merci bien et Dieu te beni.* Celebrate the beginnings. . . .

And to Janice Thompson, aka Janice the Magnificent, who critiqued this manuscript faster than I wrote it. Long may you rule!

Finally, to my children, Josh and Andrew, who are Cajuns by birth, and Jacob and Hannah, who are Texans for the same reason. Like Cleo and Tante Flo, I *do* love my babies! You are *my* heroes!

A note from the Author:
I love to hear from my readers! You may correspond with me by writing:

Kathleen Miller Y'Barbo
Author Relations
PO Box 719
Uhrichsville, OH 44683

ISBN 1-59310-633-5

BAYOU BEGINNINGS

All scripture quotations are taken from the King James Version of the Bible.

Our mission is to publish and distribute inspirational products offering exceptional value and biblical encouragement to the masses.

PRINTED IN THE U.S.A.

author's note

Wherever possible, I have inserted a bit of the native language of the Louisiana Acadians. A spoken language rather than a written one, Cajun French—as the language is known—is a blend of proper French, African influences, Indian words, and local dialect. The language has been passed down by word of mouth over generations and thus can vary slightly from one community to the next among the bayou people. A dictionary of common Cajun French phrases has been provided at the end of this novel. Any mistake is mine alone.

Guide to Conversational Cajun French

Allons – Let's go
Arête – Stop
Bonjour – Good morning
Bonsoir – Good evening
Ça va bien, merci – I am fine, thank you
C'est moi – It's me
C'est tout – That's all
Cher – Dear or darling
Comment ça va? – How's it going?
Dieu te beni – God bless you
Je t'aime – I love you
Le bon Dieu – The good Lord
Madame – A married woman
Mademoiselle – An unmarried woman or girl
Merci – Thank you
Merci beaucoup – Thank you very much
Mes ami(s) – My friend(s)
Monsieur – A man
Pas du tout – Not at all
Quoi y'a – What's wrong?
Sa fini pas – It never ends
Sa te regard pas – It doesn't concern you
Vien ici – Come here

one

Latagnier, Louisiana—March 1904

Most days, the effort not to eavesdrop proved too much for Clothilde Trahan, especially when the pastor came to call. It was a sin, and she knew it, but the Lord *had* made her curious. Knowing the difference between inquisitive and nosey, however, was an ongoing project.

Then there was the problem of speaking her mind when good sense and proper raising told her she ought not. It did keep her busy, this effort to keep her ears and her mouth from causing her grief.

Just about the only time she stayed out of trouble was when she had her nose in one of Uncle Joe's or Tante Flo's books. Fortunately, her adopted parents—the childless sister and brother-in-law to her late mother—valued a good book over almost anything except *the* Good Book. Quick to catch on, Cleo soon found books became the friends she would otherwise not have in this isolated area of the Bayou Nouvelle.

Funny thing. This time books just might be the cause of the problem.

"I declare, *mon ami*, it's a crying shame," she heard the reverend say. "There ought to be something we can do about it."

Cleo leaned closer to the parlor doors, keeping the dust rag moving along the cypress wainscoting in case Tante Flo might quietly wander down from her afternoon nap. For her uncle to close the parlor doors on a Tuesday afternoon meant something big was afoot. It also meant he didn't want her listening.

But to what?

"I agree with you, Joe. I can't tell you how many letters I've written, and nothing seems to come of it. The powers that be up in New Orleans, well, they got bigger fish to fry."

The reverend used his Sunday voice, the loud, insistent one that called for action rather than the softer thank-you-for-the-dinner-invitation version she generally heard outside the churchyard. Another reason for concern.

"Even if we could manage a way around the *how* of it, we'd still have to find a place to hold the classes. And then there's the problem of the teacher. Have you had any luck?"

"I sent a few letters," Uncle Joe said, "but so far there's been no one willing to quit a sure job teaching to come take a chance on a town with no schoolhouse and no money to pay a teacher."

Cleo let the rag hang limp in her hand. Realization dawned. The school. They were talking about it again.

For all the folks who called Latagnier home, there was much to recommend the little place. Good food and good friends, that's what bayou folks made. But for all the common sense the people of her adopted home held, few had the book learning to go along with it.

To be sure, Uncle Joe had been educated over in New Orleans, but he was one of the rare few. He'd met and married Tante Flo there and taken her from the schoolroom where she presided to the home where they still lived today.

No doubt in the beginning Tante had expected she would fill the rooms of this place with babies to make up for the children she'd turned over to another teacher at the end of the term. Instead, the cradles were never filled. Not once. At least not until Cleo came to live with them at the age of three.

But that was a story unto itself, fifteen years in the past and not worthy of consideration when an event such as the one going on behind the parlor doors was occurring.

Through the tiny crack in the sliding doors, Cleo could barely make out the shape of the pastor sitting beside the fireplace in the stiff, horsehair chair. Gesturing while leaning forward, he reminded Cleo of the funny little praying mantis she had caught on the screen just yesterday.

Although she could not see him, she knew Uncle Joe would be across from him, probably perching his wiry self on the edge of the rosewood divan. Between them would be the remains of a plate of cookies alongside two of Tante Flo's teacups, a wedding gift from the New Orleans side of the family and brought out only on special occasions: Christmas, anniversaries, birthdays, and visits from Pastor Broussard. With Uncle Joe being an elder, the pastor's visits were the most common.

Cleo let the pretense and the rag drop. "Of course. The teacups." She smiled and bustled toward the summer kitchen to put water on to boil. Where were her manners?

An eternity later, the big pot had boiled, and she wrapped a thick towel around its handle and headed for the parlor. "More tea," she said as she pushed the doors aside and barged in. Avoiding Uncle Joe's gaze, she centered her efforts on acting the hostess Tante Flo had trained her to be. *"Bonjour,* Pastor Broussard. Sugar?" she asked as she set the tray aside and poured steaming water into the pot.

"Bonjour, Mademoiselle Trahan."

"Clothilde," Uncle Joe said.

One word. Many meanings. None good. She braved a look. Did she detect a smile?

"I wondered when you'd find a way in here. I'm sure the wall outside the door shines like a new penny."

Cleo felt the color rise in her cheeks. "Why, Uncle Joe, whatever are you talking about? I'm just doing my chores like Tante Flo asked."

"The Lord loves a busy body," the reverend said. "And that's two words, not one."

"Yes, sir," she said softly.

Uncle Joe settled back on the divan and grinned. "Remind me to tell Flo there's more to dusting the hallway than just that little section beside the parlor door she told you to concentrate on." He winked at Cleo. "Now along with you, *cher*. The reverend and I have business to conduct."

"Oui," she said under her breath, all the while wishing she had the gall to plop down on the divan beside her uncle and tell them exactly how they could solve the problem of finding a place for the local schoolhouse.

She took her time collecting the items to take back to the kitchen. Just when she thought the men would never resume their conversation, the pastor set down his teacup. "I declare, Joe, we're in the business of saving souls, but we ought to do something for them while they're waiting for Glory, don't you think?"

Cleo gathered up the tray and pretended to study the door. She walked as slowly as she could, but still she traversed the distance far too quickly.

"I agree," Uncle Joe said. "But even if we could find a place to hold classes until we raise the money for a decent schoolhouse, who in the world would we get to teach the children?"

The old building in the corner of the property, she longed to say. *Fix it and fill it with children, and I'll teach them.* Instead, she clamped down on her tongue, tucked the tray under her arm, and shoved open the parlor door.

"Clothilde Trahan, *vien ici*. Where have you got off to?" Tante Flo's voice coiled through the room and made Cleo cringe. Her aunt would have her hide for sure if she found her bothering the menfolk.

"Coming." Cleo failed to reach the hallway before Tante Flo barged through, nearly upsetting the pan of hot water.

Tiny in stature but with a smile that radiated larger-than-life love, Cleo's aunt now wore just the opposite—an uncharacteristic frown. "What have you been up to, child?"

"Flo, come on in here and say hello to Pastor," Uncle Joe called. Tante Flo turned to offer Uncle Joe and the reverend a greeting, then cast a glance back at Cleo. Her smile had nearly returned. Nearly, but not quite. "You get along with yourself now and leave the men be."

Cleo looked past her aunt to the men who watched the exchange with amused faces. "Pleasure to see you again, sir," she said to the pastor.

"Flo, you were a teacher once," Cleo heard the reverend say as she stepped into the hall. "Joe and I were just discussing the problem we're having finding someone to take on the teaching of the children once we get ourselves a building."

Carefully setting the pan of water on the sideboard, Cleo tiptoed back to the hallway. She'd been giving the problem of the local school much thought on her morning walks to the bayou, and just last week she'd come upon what she thought might be the perfect solution. If only she could find a way of telling Uncle Joe besides just barging in and stating her case.

"Oh, I just couldn't." Cleo leaned out of her hiding place to see Tante Flo sitting next to Uncle Joe on the divan. "It's just not done, Joe. *Pas du tout*," she said, shaking her head. "I'm a married woman, and I haven't seen the inside of a schoolhouse in nigh on twenty years. I can't teach those children. Besides, we don't even have money for a place yet."

"Oh, we've got a little bit saved. Enough to get things started," the pastor said. "The rest'll come. I just know it will."

Uncle Joe clutched his wife's hand. "The reverend and I are believing the Lord for both a teacher and a place to teach. The need is so great, what with all these young 'uns coming up. I just know He will bring someone forward who has the answers."

"I have the answers." Cleo pressed her fingers to her mouth and felt the heat rise in her cheeks. Had she actually spoken the words aloud?

"Clothilde Trahan," Tante Flo said. "Are you eavesdropping again?"

Cleo stood stock-still. What to say?

"*Vien ici*, young lady."

Come here? Uh oh. Uncle Joe's firm voice. Cleo tried to convince her feet to either flee or obey but found them as stuck as if she were up to her knees in bayou mud.

Her gaze first met Tante Flo's, then locked with her uncle's. Neither looked pleased.

"I'm sorry," she mumbled. "I'll just go on back to the kitchen."

"Come here, child," the reverend said. She shifted her attention to him. At least he wore a smile. "I would like to hear what Clothilde has to say. What plan have you brought us? Will you be telling us how to build our schoolhouse or where to find a teacher?"

Rather than attempt to move, Cleo lowered her eyes and studied the roses on the carpet. "Actually, sir, I may have the solution to both."

She watched their faces as she let the long pent-up words spill forth. When she'd finished detailing all the fine attributes of the run-down cottage at the edge of her uncle's property, she said a little prayer and plunged forward with the finest idea of all.

"And I will be the teacher."

Cleo clamped her mouth shut, then paused to offer a weak smile. The silence in the room roared louder than last summer's Fourth of July tornado. Did they sit in stunned silence at the audacity of the plan, or had her idea been such a good one that they needed a moment to wrap their minds around it?

The pastor leaned forward to rest bony elbows on bonier knees. Neither Tante Flo nor Uncle Joe moved a muscle.

Outside the parlor window, a crow cackled, then swooped toward Tante Flo's vegetable garden. The bird had become the first to laugh at her plan but obviously would not be the last.

"You know, Joe," the reverend said, "Clothilde just might have something there."

Cleo let out the breath she'd been holding. She shifted her gaze to her aunt and uncle.

"You think so, Reverend?" Uncle Joe cast a sideways glance at Tante Flo. "We always said we'd fix that old place up or let it be torn down, one or the other, but I never got to it."

Tante Flo nodded. "Nothing but a home for mice and the occasional cottonmouth. Do you think it's worth fixing, Joe? I mean, we don't want the children in a building that's going to fall down around their precious heads."

"The old place is as sound as it gets. My granddaddy's daddy built it to last. Not even old General Sherman could tear it down. It wouldn't take half the money we've set aside to turn it into a proper schoolhouse." Uncle Joe hit his knees with his fists. "You know, Pastor, I think my girl just might have something here."

He rested his head in his hands as if in prayer, then lifted his gaze to smile at Uncle Joe. "I do believe she might."

A moment later, the men were embroiled in animated conversation, each topping the other on the improvements that could be made to the modest cottage, until Uncle Joe shook his head. "You know, the only thing is, the men of the church, we're farmers and trappers. We've got the know-how to make this place shine, but we just don't have the time. It'll take an eternity to get all of this work done unless we hire the biggest part of it out."

"You're right, Joe," the reverend said. "And I believe I just might have the man for the job."

two

Theophile Breaux leaned back against the porch rail and studied the moss-covered trees dotting the horizon. A chill wind blew across the porch and settled in his soul. All the while, birds chirped a rhythm old as the water flowing silently past the eastern edge of the Breaux property. Somewhere beyond the cypress and pines and the Bayou Nouvelle lay that big old world Theo loved so much.

Ever since he could remember, he'd been on a path leading out of town. He'd been knee high to a grasshopper when he first saw how hard his papa worked and how little he got for the hides he took to town. Way back then, Theo had made a promise to himself and the Lord.

Well, actually it was more of a deal.

If Theo obeyed his mama and papa and did all the things the Good Book said, the Lord would give him a life free from toil and trials. So far, so good. He'd all but made good his escape, having been gone from the old home place the better part of three years before Papa slipped and fell on a patch of late-season ice.

Mama'd tracked Theo down through the big network of family spread across Louisiana and Texas. A telegram arrived on the doorstep of his rooming house in Houston just about the time Theo was thinking of saying good-bye to his Texas kin and heading north to Oklahoma or maybe up to Canada.

He smiled. Perhaps someday his travels would lead him to Grand Pre in Nova Scotia, where his kin, the original Acadians, once called home.

Now wouldn't that be something? This old Cajun sitting

pretty in the place where his great-great-great-granddaddy wasn't welcome.

His smile deepened and turned to a chuckle. Funny how he thought of himself as old. While he was the eldest of the bunch, he still had a few years to go before he would see thirty.

Off in the distance, the younger children played a game of some sort, and across the way, his sisters washed clothes in the bayou's rolling waters. Bessie beat one of Mama's white aprons on a rock, while Addie worked a pair of Papa's trousers across the rub board. Somewhere along the bayou, Alphonse and Pete checked the traps, and in the house, Lucy and Kate helped Mama strip the beds. In the summer kitchen, Alouise and Jeannine would be starting the gumbo that would simmer until suppertime.

Closing his eyes, he could see it all. The faces of his brothers and sisters eventually replaced by their children and their children's children, just as it had been in the centuries since government orders sent the Acadians spilling down the Mississippi into south Louisiana. Nothing had changed in the bayou, and it never would.

Sa fini pas. It never ends.

"By your age I'd been married to your mama for a coon's age and was raising a houseful of young 'uns," Papa had told him over coffee just this morning. "Your time's a-comin', son. The Lord's about to let you meet your match."

"Must be your broke bone you feel it in," he'd joked. But standing here with the sounds of the bayou swirling around him, the joke fell flat. If he didn't get out of here soon, he just might fall into the same trap that bound Papa to the muddy land. Then what?

Theo turned up the collar of his heavy shirt and shifted from the shadows into the warmth of the sunshine. Foolishness, this idea he might get hung up here indefinitely. He and the Lord had a deal. The road had detoured for just a bit, but he'd soon be back on it. Daddy's broken leg was healing nicely, and Mama said he'd be back to trapping in no time.

The faster the better, to Theo's way of thinking, because he had plans. He loved his mama and daddy, but nothing set his teeth on edge worse than being stuck in a small place with a big number of relatives.

With one kinfolk shy of a dozen, the old house overflowed.

"Theo, you'll be back in time for supper?"

He turned to grin at his mother. Careworn yet wearing a smile, she stood in the doorway with a set of bed linens draped over one arm.

"*Oui*, Mama," he said. "I aim to see that place the reverend told me about, and then I'll head on back home. Don't 'spect it'll take more'n a few hours unless I get a mind to catch a fish or two."

She shook her head and clutched the bleached white sheets to her chest. "Fishing, that's a man's excuse for sittin' still. You tell the reverend he's overdue for a gumbo supper, and I aim to set an extra place this evenin'. If he's a mind t'join us, he knows he don't need no engraved invitation."

"I will." Mama wouldn't know an engraved invitation if it slapped her upside the head, but she sure liked to use that term. "Theophile, you know you can come home any time you want. You don't need no engraved invitation." He'd asked her once if she had any idea what she was talking about. She'd responded with a comment about how sassy he'd become since he no longer lived under her roof, then stormed off.

He'd hoped to talk her and Papa into visiting him in Houston, but it never happened. There was always something that kept them stuck here. Well, when he got himself a little place up in Canada, he'd send them all train tickets.

Theo watched Mama climb the wooden steps leading from the front porch up into the attic space where the boys slept.

Years ago, he'd offered to build an inside staircase. The old tax laws that forced the Acadians to get creative with their living spaces were no longer in force, making the outside stairway unnecessary. Still, Mama and Papa refused the change, preferring instead to go out on the porch in order to reach the upper half of the house.

One more example of how things never seemed to change on the bayou.

He turned east toward the Trahan place. Whatever the reverend had to show him, it ought to be more interesting than what went on around here.

Tromping through the marsh, he fell into his habit of conversing with the Lord. Generally a one-sided conversation with him doing all the talking and God doing all the listening, the prayer this afternoon involved Theo merely asking a single question—when his time in Latagnier would be done—and then waiting in silence for an answer.

This is your home. It will never be done, came the soft reply.

Stopping short, Theo looked up toward the cornflower blue sky and squinted. "Lord, did I hear You right? I'm *never* leaving Latagnier? Well, I just don't think I'm gonna believe that."

He stomped his boots to shake off the remains of yesterday's walk through the muddy bayou's edge, then shielded his eyes from the sun. If only he could shield them from the Son, as well. That, Theo knew, was useless. The Lord saw everything; He just acted like He didn't sometimes.

Like now. Couldn't God see he wanted to be free of the life that broke his daddy's spirit and sent him to carrying an old man's load at a young man's age?

What if the load was not a burden?

Again the Father's voice teased his ears and pierced his heart. He'd never considered Papa might actually *like* the lot he'd been cast.

"What if I mean for you to carry the same load?"

"I won't do it, I tell You," he muttered. "I just can't."

"That you, Theo?" The Reverend Broussard stood some hundred yards away, waving his arms.

"Oui, c'est moi." Theo returned the greeting and stomped toward him. Where did a man go for an appeal when the Creator of the universe handed down a verdict he didn't like? Even the reverend wouldn't have an answer to that one.

He shook off the thought and plowed forward through the mucky ground until he hit the hard-packed earth. By that time, the reverend stood only a few yards away. *"Bonjour, Reverend,"* he said as he closed the distance between them. *"Comment ça va?"*

"Things are going well, son. Thank you for asking." The reverend adjusted his hat, then shook Theo's hand. "Pleasure seeing you on a day besides Sunday. I'm glad you've chosen to stay here in Latagnier for a while."

This parson, different from others Theo had come across, had calluses that bore the signs of a workingman's life. Like the rest of the men in Latagnier, he worked hard for his living, saving souls on Sunday and tilling the land the rest of the week.

"Well, not me," Theo said softly as he shoved his fists into his pockets and looked away.

"Excuse me?" the reverend asked.

Theo shook his head. "Nothing," he said as he turned his attention to the ramshackle pile of boards and windows gathering leaves—and most likely snakes—beside the little cabin. Many years ago, the structure had been someone's home, but now it sat empty and forgotten. "So this is the place you're thinking of turning into a schoolhouse, eh?"

The preacher nodded. "What do you think?"

His carpenter's eye told him there was hope in the little structure. His heart, however, said there was much more to life than staying as long as fixing up this place would take.

three

Now don't you go bothering the menfolks, Clothilde Trahan. You hear?" Tante Flo stood at the back door, tiny hands on narrow hips. Her frown spoke more than her warning. "I want you to promise me."

"I promise." *I won't bother them. They'll never know I'm around.*

"Some folks, they can't help the way God made 'em. They just go on about their business without thinking what they're doing might be their downfall." Tante Flo shook her head. "Honey, I know you're curious, but you're also a lady, and a lady knows when to make herself scarce."

"I don't know what you're talking about." As Cleo said the words, she knew she could offer no proof. On the other hand, Tante Flo had caught her spying too many times to count.

Tante Flo placed her hand over Cleo's. "Someday you're gonna have a house full of young 'uns, and at least one of 'em's gonna be just like you. More and more every day, you're becoming like your mama, God rest her precious soul."

Cleo looked into the eyes of the dear woman who'd raised her. "I am?"

"You are. Look just like her, too. If the fever hadn't taken her and your papa, well. . ." Tante Flo looked away. For a moment she seemed lost in memories. Then she straightened her shoulders and clapped her hands. "Enough of this foolishness. You and me, we got work to do. *Allons!* Get me plenty of eggs then, chile. I've got to make pies enough for tomorrow's church social and Sunday dinner, too."

"Yes, ma'am." Cleo slipped her arm through the handle of

the egg basket and turned in the direction of the henhouse. Uncle Joe hadn't exactly forbidden her to go out to the site where the men were meeting, and neither had Tante Flo. Her only promise had been the one she had just made, and to the best of her ability, she meant to keep her pledge.

Buster, Uncle Joe's ancient Catahoula cur hound, trotted over to wag his tail and sniff at the basket. "Nothing in here for you, Buster," she said. "But I could use some company. *Allons!* Come on, and let's go get Tante Flo some eggs for her pies."

Feeling her aunt's watchful eyes boring into her back, Cleo headed for the chicken house with the dog on her heels. The basket swung from her elbow and slapped against her side as she traveled the short distance to reach the henhouse door. Casting a glance over her shoulder, she saw Tante Flo still standing in the doorway.

"Well, I suppose I'm going to have to go inside," she said under her breath. The hound, nose to the ground, headed off in pursuit of some unknown quarry.

Cleo stepped inside the dank warmth of the henhouse and blinked to adjust her eyes to the dimness. The birds began to fuss and cluck as she went about the business of collecting the day's eggs as slowly as she could manage.

When she'd gathered the last egg, she cautiously pushed the door open and peered outside. No one stood nearby. Even the dog had disappeared.

She craned her neck to get a better look at the back door and the open windows along the back of the house. No sight of Tante Flo.

Cleo set the egg basket on the floor of the henhouse and darted toward the stand of trees shielding the bayou from sight. Once she slipped into the shadows of the thicket, it was a simple matter to stroll casually along the bank. If anyone saw her, she'd easily make the excuse that she'd followed the bayou where the bayou led, taking the fresh air on her daily stroll.

Funny how the bayou seemed to be leading right toward the prospective schoolhouse.

"I don't know, Reverend. It looks like we can save most of that wood if we. . ." The voice faded and disappeared as Cleo neared the site. The reverend and his carpenter friend must have gone inside the cabin to check things out.

No matter. She could wait. But first, perhaps she should make sure they truly were inside.

Cleo crept toward the cabin, being careful to keep out of sight of the lone window on the easternmost corner of the building. She moved slowly, a difficult thing for her, until she reached the side of the cabin. From that point, she began to make her way around the edge of the house, hoping to reach the front in time to see the men exit.

"I see what you mean," the reverend said from somewhere nearby. "What do you think, Joe?"

The window. Cleo looked up to see she stood directly beneath it. She cowered against the side of the house and tried not to breathe, all the while willing the men to move so she could do the same.

"Theo, if we were to take out that wall, would it hurt the integrity of the structure?"

The carpenter's rumbling voice answered in the affirmative. "But Joe, if you'll look over here, I think it can be done this way. See what you think, eh?"

"You know," the reverend said, "I think Theo might just be on the right track."

All three voices moved away from the window and faded into silence. Leaning against the rough wood, Cleo expelled a long breath to still her racing heart.

She'd been spared the humiliation of being caught listening, but with the sounds of the men's voices drawing near once more, her reprieve was only a temporary solution. If she stayed in the clearing, she'd be found out for sure.

"Let me show the window casing on the back of the house," Uncle Joe said, his voice too near for comfort. *"Vien ici."*

Casting a glance over her shoulder, she realized the only way to leave was to go the same way she came. Saying a quick prayer, Cleo darted toward the thicket and dove into the stand of pines. She landed with a thud in a pile of pine needles, then rolled over and lay face down. Peering up, she held her breath while three sets of male legs filed past just a few yards away.

A mosquito buzzed her ears, and no matter how hard she tried, Cleo couldn't get rid of the pesky thing. Swatting it was out of the question—too loud—and enduring it for five more minutes was more than she could consider. Thankfully, none of the other bayou creatures had joined her—yet.

As she watched the backs of the men, heads bent in conversation over a paper the reverend held, Cleo's mind began to conjure up all the possibilities for animal and reptile companions. Behind her, the pine straw rustled, while overhead a black crow screeched, seemingly determined to give away her hiding space.

She had to do something.

Cleo inched closer to the clearing where the reverend stood side by side with the stranger. He was a tall man, this Acadian whom the reverend had chosen to do the cabin repairs. Dark arms emerged from beneath rolled-up shirtsleeves, proclaiming him a man who'd spent time in the sun.

Uncle Joe said he was a Breaux, the oldest of the bunch and the only one who no longer lived on the bayou. Cleo closed her eyes, trying to remember him, then opened them quickly when the mosquito struck again.

From her hiding place in the thicket, she could barely make out the top of the fellow's dark head as he disappeared behind the structure with the pastor on his heels.

"Hey there, Joe," she heard the reverend call. A muted response drifted her way. So did a familiar bark.

Oh no.

Suppressing a groan, Cleo gathered her skirts around her legs and crouched lower. She tried to force herself to breathe slowly, but the effort made her dizzy. If Uncle Joe caught her eavesdropping again, she'd surely end up riling him. The last thing she needed in her campaign to be chosen as the first teacher of the new school was to upset one of the men who would be doing the choosing.

Another bark, this one closer.

Buster.

Cleo suppressed a groan and gathered her skirt and apron close beneath her. Wouldn't you know the dog with the greatest tracking sense in the parish would show up now?

Uncle Joe called the hound by name, then knelt as the Catahoula cur bounded into the clearing. Unfortunately, Buster did not head toward Uncle Joe, but rather stopped abruptly a few yards away, then turned in her direction.

Nose to the ground, he made short work of crossing the distance to where Cleo cowered in the thicket. "Go away," she whispered. "*Allons!* Get out of here."

"What you got there, Buster?" Uncle Joe called, his voice coming closer. "You got a rabbit?"

"A nosey rabbit. Now go on," she said under her breath as she slid farther back into her hiding place and laid her head on the blanket of pine needles. Again, the mosquito buzzed her ear, but she dared not swat it.

The dog continued to press his way through the thick branches to bury his wet nose in the top of Cleo's head. His whimper turned into a full-fledged bark.

"Here now, Buster," Uncle Joe called. "*Vien ici.* Leave that little rabbit alone."

Buster hesitated and barked once more. Cleo lifted her head and swatted his nose, sending him running. She inched forward a bit to watch him launch himself at Uncle Joe.

"Did it get you, boy?" Uncle Joe knelt to ruffle the dog's ears. "You want me to go catch him and put him in the stew pot?"

Cleo sucked in a deep breath and held it until Uncle Joe stood and turned away. In one quick motion, she let out her breath and swatted the mosquito.

Uncle Joe stopped in his tracks and whirled around. He peered in the direction of Cleo's hiding place, then shook his head and motioned to Buster. *"Allons,* hound dog. You and me got some work to do back at the house. You coming, men?"

The reverend nodded and joined Uncle Joe, but the Breaux fellow motioned them away. "I believe I'll stay here a bit longer if you don't mind."

Uncle Joe smiled. "All right, but before we go, I need to know if you'll change your mind about taking payment for this, Theo. It's not right you doing all that work for nothing."

The Breaux fellow stepped into Cleo's view. *Oh my. He did turn out to be quite handsome. And tall, too.* When he looked over in the direction of the thicket, her heart skipped, only in part from fear of being discovered.

The carpenter said something, then turned and headed back toward the cabin, disappearing inside. Cleo plucked a piece of pine straw from her hair and wished for a comb. "What am I thinking? I won't be meeting him today. He can't know I've been spying."

Did she say spying? Well, actually she'd been. . .the truth was, she'd actually wanted to. . .see, she just needed to know. . . .

Cleo sighed. She'd been spying, all right. The reverend was right. God loved a busy body but not a busybody.

She sat back in her hiding space and tucked her knees beneath her chin, wrapping her arms around her legs. A big ugly water bug skittered past and disappeared into the straw, and she kicked at it with the toe of her shoe. Right at that moment, Cleo felt like that ugly bug.

Stretching out her legs, she leaned back against the rough bark of the nearby pine. She closed her eyes, her heart heavy.

I'm sorry, Lord. Please forgive me for snooping again. Teach me to keep my nose in my own business. I'm ready to accept the consequences, but be gentle while I learn.

Before she could say "amen," she felt something cool and heavy slither across her legs. The operative word was *slither*. When she opened her eyes, a big old cottonmouth lay across her ankles.

The snake looked almost as unhappy to see her as she was to see him.

four

Theo climbed onto an abandoned kitchen chair and studied the old building's rafters. Joe was right when he said the place stood as sturdy as the day it was built. Planed smooth and straight by hands long stilled in death, the wood held true and plumb. A job well done. Only the cobwebs that hung like Spanish moss in the corners gave away its age.

He stretched to reach the nearest cypress beam, then ran his hand over the aged timber. Nothing felt more permanent than a piece of wood well crafted.

"Help! Snake!"

The chair tumbled from beneath him as Theo tried to right himself. He landed with a crash and hit the ground running. As he careened off the porch, he grabbed the shovel off the top of the lumber pile.

"Where are you?"

"Over here!"

Following the sound, Theo crossed the clearing and bounded into the thicket only to stop short when he saw the woman—and the woman's predicament. A rather small-sized female had attracted a big old snake. It sat on the hem of her skirt, mad as a hornet and perched to strike.

Theo smacked the ground with the shovel, and the black monster turned his attention away from the young lady. As soon as the snake moved, so did the woman. Using the tip of the shovel, Theo made short work of the cottonmouth. With a flick of his wrist, he sent the head flying into the thicket and watched it land, then bounce into the black water of the bayou.

When he glanced back at the terrified woman, he had to suppress a groan. She stared down at the twitching body of the snake as if she'd never seen one. The only thing worse than a riled-up cottonmouth was a riled-up woman.

And this one looked ready to strike.

Mouth covered by shaking hands, the woman began to cry. "I asked Him to be gentle, and He sent a snake." She swiped at her tears with the hem of her apron, then thrust her hand toward him with a weak smile. "I'm sorry. My name is Clothilde, Clothilde Trahan. How do you do?"

"Theophile Breaux." He handed her his handkerchief. "You must be Joe's girl."

"Oui," she said as she dabbed at her cheeks. "I'm his niece."

He shook her hand. She sure was a pretty little thing. No bigger than a minute and covered in pine straw, yet he couldn't recall when he'd seen anyone more appealing. He frowned. Last thing he needed was a distraction, and this brown-eyed beauty sure looked to be one. With little encouragement, he just might fall in love, and then where would he be?

Just like his papa, that's where.

Focus, Breaux. Think of something besides her broad smile and that upturned nose.

What had she said about the snake? That someone sent it? Was she loony? Joe had mentioned his niece was a bit of a challenge, but he never stated specifically what he meant.

"What are you talking about? Who sent a snake?"

"God, I think." She spared another quick look at the twitching remains before meeting his gaze. Her lower lip quivered a bit, but at least her tears had stopped. "You see, I know God corrects us when we do wrong, and I was. . ."

Theo jammed the point of the shovel into the soft earth, then leaned on the handle. They were heading for dangerous territory. She'd been watching him from the thicket, and now he couldn't take his eyes off her. A gentleman, especially one in a hurry to get on down the road, would walk away right now and leave the lady to her concerns.

Well, he'd rarely been accused of doing what he ought. What was the harm in just a little more conversation while he watched the sun glint off her blue-black hair?

"You were *what*?" he asked with a mind to tease just a bit before he sent her home to her uncle.

"I was. . ." Her face colored the prettiest shade of pink. "Well, never mind what I was doing."

"You were eavesdropping."

She had the decency to appear ashamed. *"Oui,"* she said slowly, "I was."

"You were hiding in the thicket, listening to everything we said." He gave her the look he generally reserved for his younger brothers and sisters. "I should tell your uncle."

Brown eyes opened wide. "I wish you wouldn't."

Rather than respond, he decided to say nothing and watch her squirm.

She offered a weak smile. "I have a good reason."

"A good reason to do something wrong?" He leaned down to look her in the eyes. "Is that what you're trying to tell me?"

"Yes. I mean no." She worried with the hem of her apron. "You see, I thought maybe I. . . Oh, goodness."

"Goodness has got nothing to do with it, girl." He tilted forward slightly and noted with satisfaction that the Trahan girl took a step back. "Was what you heard worth nearly getting snakebit?"

She shook her head.

"Was it worth whatever your uncle's going to do when he hears about this?"

Again she shook her head. "No, but you don't understand. If you tell him, it will ruin everything."

There went the tears. Theo groaned. This girl shed more liquid than a rowboat with a plank missing.

Be strong, Breaux. Just walk away.

Of course, he ignored his own advice. "If I don't tell your uncle, you'll probably keep sticking your nose where it doesn't belong until you run into something—or someone—worse than that snake there."

"I think I already have."

Theo grasped the end of the shovel and yanked hard to pull it out of the dirt. Slinging it over his shoulder, he turned and walked away.

⁂

Why didn't she keep her big mouth shut?

Cleo stepped over the carcass of the snake and headed after the Breaux fellow. If only she could make him see his way clear to keep quiet on her little indiscretion. Indiscretion? Who was she kidding? She'd blatantly ignored both her aunt and her uncle and hidden in a thicket like a common criminal, all in the hopes of learning whether or not a teacher had been chosen for the school.

She'd tried asking Tante Flo outright and Uncle Joe indirectly, but neither offered an answer as to who would be offered the task of teaching the children. Both knew she wanted the position, so repeating her wish would serve no purpose. It certainly hadn't kept Uncle Joe from sending a letter to New Orleans to the teachers' college to inquire about qualified applicants for the job.

Going to the reverend was out of the question because he would just inform Uncle Joe. If only she'd learned to take to heart some of the scriptures on patience she'd memorized through the years.

Cleo watched the broad back of the man who could single-handedly ruin her plans for the future. *Stop him, Lord. Please.*

Abruptly the man halted and whirled around to face her. "Get on home, little girl."

Little girl? When would people see her as a full-grown

woman of almost nineteen? Her uncle and aunt certainly didn't, or they wouldn't be ignoring her requests to hire on as a teacher for the bayou school. And this man. . .

Well, she would show them all.

She drew herself up to her full height and stalked toward Theophile Breaux. "Little girl?" she called as she closed the distance between them. "You think I am a little girl, Monsieur Breaux?"

By the time she asked the question, she stood inches away from him. He leaned toward her as if to study her a moment, then crossed his arms over his chest. A broad grin split his handsome face, and he broke out into laughter.

Laughter.

Cleo felt the heat flood her face. How *dare* he laugh at her? If she hadn't been brought up to be a lady, she would certainly wipe the smile off his face with a choice word or two. Instead, she merely stood her ground and endured the humiliation until the Breaux fellow finally tired of his fun.

"Are you quite finished?" she asked as properly as she could.

The Breaux fellow's face sobered, but traces of the grin remained. "I suppose I am."

"Then may I ask you a question?"

He looked stunned. "I suppose so."

"What will you accomplish by telling my uncle you found me out here?"

"Accomplish?" The Acadian seemed to consider the question a moment. "I don't rightly know. You got the answer to that, eh?"

"Then don't tell him." She made an attempt to smile. "I have such plans, and all you will do is ruin them."

"Well, of all the. . ." He shook his head. "You mean to try and tell me that even though you are in the wrong, I'm the one who'll cause trouble by telling the truth? Little girl, you are something. Did you know that?" With those words, he turned and stormed away, crossing the distance to the cabin's front porch with angry steps that raised little clouds of dust on the dry ground.

"I was just trying to figure out if they'd hired a teacher," she called. "And you can believe that or not."

"Why would you care about a teacher?" he asked without breaking his stride or looking her way. "You might be little bitty, but I know you're past school age." He glanced over his shoulder as he stomped up the porch steps. "At least I think you are, but then now that I—"

His leg disappeared into the porch step up to his knee. Catching the rail, he narrowly missed falling forward onto the porch. The big man leaned precariously against the rail, unable to lift his leg out of the crumbled wood that held it imprisoned.

"Are you all right?" Cleo picked up her skirts and raced toward the struggling man, climbing past him to stand on the porch. She offered her outstretched hand. "Here. Let me help."

Gratitude was *not* written on his face as he looked up at her. "What in the world can a little thing like you do to help me, eh?"

"You never can tell." She tried not to laugh at the bits of rotten wood and dead leaves decorating his dark curls. "Uncle Joe says I'm stronger than I look. I'll pull, and you try to lift your foot over those boards."

She grasped his hand and tugged. A moment later, he caught his balance. Unfortunately, she lost hers, tangled her feet in her skirts, and landed with a thud on her posterior.

The Breaux fellow completed his climb out of the rotten stairs, then pulled himself up on the porch beside her. He shook his head, and leaves and wood chips fell like the snowflakes in Tante Flo's snow globe all around him, some decorating the hem of her skirt.

For a moment she thought he might see some humor in the situation. The wind kicked up, sending another shower of debris her way. She offered a smile in anticipation of the return of his good humor.

Return? When did she actually see any of it? A glance up at the frown on his face told her it would not be today.

What a shame that such a handsome man had such a sour disposition.

The object of her thoughts lumbered to his feet and reached for her hand, practically sending her airborne as he pulled her to a standing position. To his credit, he held her steady until she could regain her footing.

"Get on home now," he said as he released his grip.

Cleo hesitated a moment before pressing past him to carefully make her way across the rickety porch. Head held high, she stepped onto solid ground and walked away from the most irritating man she'd ever met.

five

You go tell your uncle what you've been up to, little girl, or I will," Theo called after her. "Hurry on now, or I just might get there before you. You wouldn't want that, now would you, eh?"

Clothilde Trahan just kept on walking at the same leisurely pace, back straight and head up like she was counting the clouds. If he hadn't seen the high color in her cheeks as she walked away, he would have thought she was out for a Sunday stroll.

Despite the·fact she now wore sawdust on her skirt and pine needles in her hair, she was a lady, that one, and according to his mama, raised up to be a godly woman by good people. His only memories of Clothilde Trahan were as a quiet girl forever carrying a book under her arm or hiding in some remote corner at church picnics reading while everyone else went about their foolishness. He had to admit he hadn't expected back then that she'd grow up to be quite so pretty.

Or spunky.

What was it about the Trahan girl that set his teeth on edge and his heart pumping all at the same time? Joe and his wife were the salt of the earth, and he knew they'd loved and raised that girl like she was their own.

If she'd turned out anything like her Tante Flo, she would make somebody a fine wife someday—once she let go of that nasty habit of sticking her pretty nose where it didn't belong.

Maybe she ought to go back to carrying a book around. At least then she'd have a place to stick her nose where it wouldn't get her into trouble.

He watched her disappear into the thicket and gave passing thought to whether she actually went home or stood there spying. From the look on her face when he told her he'd go to Joe, she probably hightailed it back to the house to head him off.

Scared to death, she most likely intended to give her uncle her side of the story before Theo could tell him otherwise. A fat lot of good that would do. The truth of the situation spoke for itself.

A twinge of guilt hit him hard. He shouldn't have been so rough with her. No, he decided. Served her right. A body ought not hide out like a common criminal and watch people. What in the world was she thinking?

Theo pondered on that a moment. She did have the book learning, and she knew more words than just about anybody he'd ever spoken with—and he'd talked to some really smart people in his day.

Her Tante Flo worked as a teacher way back, so the feisty gal probably got her hankering for it through her kinfolk. Yes, he could see her as a schoolteacher, at least until the little bitty thing ran across a big old bayou boy who didn't want to learn.

That last thought gave him pause. *She already has, you big fool, and she did just fine.*

Theo went back to work, taking his aggravation out on the porch steps. In short order, the rotten boards were gone, replaced by salvaged wood from the pile behind the cabin. If only he could pound away his irritation—and his thoughts of Clothilde Trahan—as easily.

❧

The following morning, Theo arrived on Joe's doorstep to discuss his ideas for the renovations. Flo welcomed him warmly. In short order, she'd hustled him into the kitchen to offer him a plate of eggs, biscuits, and bacon, which he tried and failed to turn down.

"A man's got to eat well if he's going to work well," Flo said.

"Well, I can't find an argument for that," he replied.

Joe seconded his statement with a wave of his napkin, then bowed his head to offer a blessing over the food. Fork in hand, Theo added his amen to Joe's and Flo's, then reached for the Tabasco sauce and doused everything on his plate. Satisfied he'd upped the temperature with his favorite pepper sauce, he stabbed at the bright yellow eggs and looked beyond the kitchen to the empty parlor.

Funny, here he sat at a family breakfast, and Joe's niece was nowhere to be found. He chewed on the thought—and the fiery eggs. Both burned as they went down, but only the eggs caused him to shed a tear.

Must be prettying herself up or sleeping late. No, she's probably hiding somewhere, spying.

He finished the meal and sipped good strong chicory coffee at the big round kitchen table while Flo cleared the table and then made herself scarce.

"Let's get down to business." Joe fetched a thick file off the sideboard and began to spread papers out on the table. "Tell me what you've decided we need to do."

Theo explained his ideas, all the while watching for Clothilde. He finally left, wondering where in the world the irritating woman could be.

The next morning and the one after that passed in similar fashion until the habit of starting the day with Joe and his wife fell into a routine. Theo arrived early, discussed the previous day's progress with Joe, and partook of the best coffee and eggs outside of the ones he had at his mama's house. Never had he eaten so well or sat so long at one spell.

Each time when he left, he wondered where Clothilde Trahan could be. He also promised himself each night that tomorrow he'd go straight to the building site and forgo the lollygagging at Joe's table.

Funny how he'd forget his promise every single morning. Funnier still how he figured each day would be the one when Clothilde Trahan finally stopped hiding from him.

❧

Nearly two weeks had passed, and Cleo was getting tired of missing breakfast. She stood in the henhouse with the basket hanging from her elbow. Good thing the hens were laying well.

Surely the Breaux fellow would end this annoying habit of showing up at Tante Flo's table in time to eat a half-dozen eggs and drink a gallon of coffee before finally leaving. How he could hold so much food and still maintain a lean frame baffled her further.

Must be all that work he did out at the cabin.

Still, why one man sat so long at a breakfast table was beyond her understanding. Uncle Joe did, of course, but he was old—well nigh to forty. One might expect old folks to sit and sip their coffee as if they had nothing better to do all day.

Her thoughts returned to Theophile Breaux. As far as she could tell, he hadn't informed Uncle Joe about the incident at the cabin. If he knew, Uncle Joe hadn't let on, and he certainly hadn't told Tante Flo. Perhaps the rogue had no intention of telling on her after all.

Well, wouldn't *that* be an answer to prayer?

Cleo patted her apron pocket where the letter she had written the night before lay hidden. Writing to Uncle Joe's friend at the teachers' college in New Orleans had been a risk.

She thought long and hard before resorting to the drastic move of pleading her case to a man whom she barely knew. Surely he would see her side of things when he read her letter. A man fit to run a teachers' college would obviously recognize a qualified teacher when he read a letter from one. If he wouldn't let her into the college, maybe he would recommend her to Uncle Joe as capable of teaching the children of Latagnier.

The sound of voices across the yard caught her attention.

She watched Theophile Breaux emerge from the shadows and take the front porch steps two at a time. Uncle Joe followed him out onto the porch, shouted a good-bye, and then disappeared back inside.

From experience, she knew her uncle would return to the kitchen table to work on his figuring a bit more, then take the big folder over to the church to show the reverend. After all, it *was* Friday.

Time to implement the plan she'd been working on all week. Patience was not her strong suit, but then the Lord must have known when He made her that she'd have trouble with waiting Why He chose to give her that peculiarity was something she planned to ask when she met Him someday. In the meantime, she prayed much and failed some.

This week, however, she'd managed to stick to her plan and keep her peace while she ticked off the days on the calendar. Around about Wednesday afternoon, she hadn't thought Friday would ever come, but it had.

And somehow she'd made it through the week.

Cleo plucked the last egg from the straw and settled it atop the basket. With care, she made her way out of the henhouse and up the back steps to the kitchen.

Uncle Joe sat at the table, his spectacles perched on the end of his nose and the ledger before him just as she expected. He looked up from his scribbling when the door closed.

"You been working hard this morning, *cher?*" he asked before returning his attention to his figures.

She slipped behind him to leave the egg basket on the sideboard. "Yes, sir."

He stopped writing and began tapping the tabletop with his fingers. A sure sign something was on his mind. "Seems like all that work would make a body hungry."

Cleo cringed. Enduring scrutiny from Uncle Joe hadn't been part of her expectations. "I suppose."

Had he somehow discovered that she planned to visit the postmaster on her trip to deliver eggs this morning? She cast a glance from beneath lowered lashes and found he'd gone back to his numbers.

"You want some breakfast?" he asked as he tallied a column and wrote a figure beneath it.

In truth, she did, but sitting across the table from Uncle Joe and enduring his cross-examination did not set well. An empty stomach suited her much better.

Her uncle whirled around to face her. "Any particular reason you're avoiding that young man?"

The swift change of subject startled Cleo and sent her thoughts spinning. "No, sir." She stuffed her hands into her apron pockets, then felt a pang of guilt when her fingers came into contact with her letter.

"You're not going to forget my penny candy, are you?"

Her uncle's sweet tooth was a secret to no one, but every week he felt the need to remind Cleo to fetch his favorite treat. Cleo smiled despite the worry gnawing in her gut. How she loved the familiar routine of life in Latagnier.

He stood and reached into his pocket. "Bring your aunt back one of those fancy magazines, will you?"

"Yes, sir." She accepted the coins he held out, then dropped them in her pocket alongside the letter.

Uncle Joe returned to his seat and continued to stare, all the while drumming a furious rhythm on the table. Another moment under his scrutiny and she'd spill her plan for sure.

"That you, honey?" Tante Flo called from the parlor.

Cleo suppressed a sigh of relief. "Yes, ma'am. It's me."

Tante Flo met her in the hallway, a dish towel in her hand. "You going to fetch eggs to folks?" she asked as she smoothed back iron gray hair.

"Yes'm." Cleo looked away. "Did you need something in town?"

Tossing the dish towel onto her shoulder, Tante Flo peered into Cleo's face, then pulled a letter from her apron pocket. "Mail this one with yours."

For a second Cleo could only stare at her aunt. When the words came, they emerged as more of a string of sounds rather than an actual statement of some sort. Finally, she gathered her wits enough to construct an entire sentence and speak it aloud. "How did you know?"

Tante smiled. "I didn't." She took Cleo by the elbow and led her outside. "Now don't you set your cap to worrying. I was young once, too, and I know a natural-born teacher when I see one. I just thought I ought to let that fellow at the teachers' college know, too."

Cleo opened her mouth to say thanks but once again found the words had escaped. She wrapped Tante Flo in a tight hug and held on until the tears ceased.

"Hush now and dry your eyes or your uncle's going to wonder what we hens are cackling about." She lifted the hem of her apron to dab at Cleo's tears. "Now, here's how we are going to handle this. I'll talk to your uncle, eventually, and until I do, you will keep your peace on the subject. Oh, and it wouldn't hurt to pray, too."

"I will, and I promise." Cleo kissed and hugged her aunt one more time before fairly floating to town to post not one letter to the teachers' college but two. After filling her pocket with penny candy for Uncle Joe and tucking a *Godey's Lady's Book* under her arm, she headed for home on the path that wound beside the black bayou water.

Anyone who didn't know better would think the bayou looked like a good place to spend a warm spring afternoon. Cleo knew differently, though, especially after the snake episode of last week.

She shuddered at the reminder of the black monster. While growing up on the bayou meant dealing with the ever-present snake population, she'd never seen one as large as that one.

Thoughts of the snake brought forth thoughts of the man who had dispatched it to its doom. Theophile Breaux. Now there was a man who. . .

Who what?

Before she could complete the thought, the sound of hammering echoed across the quiet of the bayou. Cleo stopped short and looked around. Had she strayed so close to the cabin that she could hear the sound of the Breaux fellow as he went about making repairs?

The familiar landmarks told her she had. Strange, but she hadn't intended to go this direction.

"Well, as long as I'm nearby, perhaps it would be a good time to see what sort of progress is being made on my school."

My school. She rolled the thought across her brain. Yes, that did sound good. And with Tante Flo's endorsement, she all but had the job sewed up.

Smiling as she headed toward the school, she toyed with the idea of letting the big Cajun know that she was the one for whom the repairs were being made. Wouldn't that just irritate him to no end?

As she reached the clearing, she cast a quick glance down at the spot where Theophile Breaux had saved her from the giant cottonmouth. Instantly she felt ashamed of herself. He really wasn't such a bad sort, just a bit grumpy and rough around the edges.

Of course, the last time she'd seen him, he'd just pulled his foot out of the steps. She looked up to see him perched atop a ladder, hammering a nail into the eaves of the cabin.

Perhaps she'd best alert him to her presence so she wouldn't startle him. A shout of greeting would probably take him by surprise, so she decided to whistle.

six

Where in the world was that infernal whistling coming from?

Theo continued to pound nails into the roof, patching places where the rain had once too often entered the little building. He'd been at it most of the morning and intended to keep going until he finished. Once the roof was in place, he could begin work inside the building.

Reaching for another nail from the pouch at his waist, Theo soon let his hands work at the task while his mind roamed. The Lord had been good to heal his papa right quick. Already he hobbled around with his leg bound up, and just yesterday he told Mama he was ready to see to his traps again.

Mama'd had a fit, of course, but soon she'd not be able to keep Papa sitting on the porch when he wanted to be out working. "A man has to work, Nellie," Theo had heard his papa say that morning. "You take a man's livelihood away, and he's got nothing."

As the screen door closed behind him, Theo heard his mama's reply, "A man's always got his family, Gaspard, and don't you ever forget that, you hear?"

Theo smiled. Nellie and Gaspard Breaux bantered like children in a schoolyard sometimes, but no one who knew them doubted their love. Thirty years of marriage come this fall, and they still held hands.

Thirty years of daily routine, of too little money and too many mouths to feed, and yet they acted like theirs had been the easiest life imaginable. He shook his head.

Papa had come back from the war with a bright future.

He'd made his plans to go east to the agricultural and mechanical college in Texas. He meant to build great things that would advance civilization.

Instead, he'd come home to the bayou to say good-bye to his mama and papa and ended up falling for Nellie Boudreaux, the pastor's daughter who'd unaccountably blossomed into womanhood during his absence.

Nellie's people were here, family with roots dug down so deep that uprooting them—and Nellie—would be unthinkable.

What in the world did a man have to do to find a woman worth giving up everything he held dear? He once asked his father that very question. His response had been characteristically vague: "I looked at Texas, I looked at Nellie, and I'll tell you, Son, Nellie looked a whole lot better. And. . ." He paused as if to draw out the moment. Theo remembered watching Papa's smile broaden then narrow as he pressed his lips into a thin line. Surely the next words out of Papa's mouth would be words of wisdom.

"And?" Theo had asked, impatient as ever.

"And besides, signs pointed to a cold winter, and it was nigh on the fall."

Mama had walked up during the middle of that statement and threatened to go after Papa with a rolling pin. Instead, the moment they thought Theo was out of sight, the pair had locked lips like newlyweds.

Theo banged another nail into the roof, then leaned back slightly on the old ladder to admire his handiwork. A neat row of shingles covered the place where a hole the size of a full-grown coon had been.

He thought about his own plans, important things to do that had been set aside for this trip to Latagnier. If he had his way, he planned to do just what he promised his papa all those years ago.

Canada. Yes, wouldn't that be something? If the pastor

hadn't roped him into this repair job, he'd practically be packing his bags. Instead, he'd bought another month or so in Latagnier, paid for with good intention and plenty of persuasion on the part of the pastor and the elders, chief among them, Joe Trahan.

Again the whistling teased his ears. No bird sang like that, at least none he'd heard in Latagnier. Leaning over, he slammed the hammer atop a nail that hadn't gone in to his liking.

There, that's better.

If a man couldn't be known for the quality of his work, well, what was the purpose of doing a job at all? It got all over him when he was called in to fix something that hadn't been done right the first time. At least that was not the case here.

"Hello? Monsieur Breaux?"

What in the world? Theo dropped his hammer onto the roof, then managed to grab it before it slid out of his reach. He turned in time to see a woman in a yellow dress emerge from the thicket. As he moved, his feet slipped, and he reached for the roof. Failing to get a grip, he settled for holding on to the only solid thing he could latch onto—the ladder.

With his heart pumping furiously, he took a deep breath and let it out slowly as he returned his attention to the work he needed to do on the roof. Releasing the ladder with a shaking left hand, he wiped the perspiration from his brow.

He'd narrowly escaped disaster this time, and he still bore the bruises from their last encounter. What was it about the Trahan woman that invited disaster each time they met? If he ignored her, maybe she'd go away, and he could leave at the end of the day without doing himself—mind or body— further damage.

"Do be careful," she called.

Several choice responses came to mind, but Mama had raised him better than to say any of them. Instead he settled for a brisk nod and a quick, "Sure will."

Once again the crooked nail caught his attention. Somehow it didn't look right anymore. He palmed the hammer and adjusted his position on the ladder. If he gave the troublesome nail a couple more hits, it would lie flat against the shingles like the others.

"That doesn't look safe, sir."

Theo jammed the hammer into his belt and cast a glance over his shoulder. She'd almost closed the distance between them, and she strolled along with a basket hanging from her elbow. The sight of her caused his mouth to go dry. If he didn't find her so irritating, he just might find her. . .what?

Attractive? Noonday sun glinted off blue-black hair that hung in a thick braid reaching nearly to her waist. Yes, he did find her quite pretty.

So what?

Pretty girls were a dime a dozen. He'd seen his share and would most likely see a good number more before Jesus called him home. Canada probably had a whole slew of them just waiting for his arrival.

So what if a girl in yellow caught his eye?

He'd be gone in no time, and she'd just be a memory. Whether she was to be a good memory or a bad one remained to be seen.

Clothilde Trahan stood at the bottom of the ladder now, and he had to lean down to see her face. "How about I do my job and you go do yours, whatever that may be, eh?"

"I *am* doing my job." She shaded her eyes and squinted up at him. "I'm going to be the teacher here, and this will be my school. As such, I felt I should come see how you were getting along."

"Your uncle and the pastor agreed to this? To you being the new teacher, that is."

She dropped her hand and looked away. "They will."

Theo chuckled. "That's what I thought. You're no more the teacher here than I am."

He whirled back around, using his left hand to steady himself as he stretched to reach the crooked nail once more. Realizing too late that he'd wiped his brow only moments before, he scrambled to keep his damp fingers wrapped around the wooden bar.

In a valiant effort to keep from sliding down the ladder, he dove for the safety of the roof. Had he been a smaller man, this might have been a good move. Unfortunately, he took after his papa's side of the family.

His last thought before crashing through the roof was that whatever happened, it would all be the Trahan woman's fault.

❧

Cleo dropped the egg basket and picked up her skirts, hurdling over the fallen ladder to reach the newly repaired porch steps. Throwing open the door, she stepped inside the semidarkness. The room smelled old and musty, and dust threatened to choke her. Obviously the carpenter's work inside had not yet commenced.

"Monsieur Breaux?"

No answer.

The cabin had been laid out in a rabbit warren of rooms, and she now stood in what remained of the largest of them. Several odd pieces of furniture—a chair here, a small table there—had been stacked into a corner, remnants of her grandmother's years living in the building.

Ahead she could see threads of light spilling around a door not quite plumb on its hinges. From memory, she knew the area where the carpenter had fallen through would be the small front room on her right. Long ago, the space had served as a formal parlor. In more recent years, it had been the sickroom for Grandmother Trahan.

Making her way carefully around the corner and into the

hallway, she stopped short at the scene unfolding before her. A brilliant shaft of light illuminated the shadowed room as if heaven itself had opened up in just one small spot. At the center of the spotlight, surrounded by a fine mist of dust, sat Theophile Breaux.

seven

The Breaux fellow had landed intact, it seemed, and unharmed and currently sat upright atop her grandmother's
ancient feather bed. Pieces of shingles and lumber littered
the bare mattress and spilled onto the old wood floor.

Covered in dust, the carpenter's dark curly hair resembled
the powdered wigs she'd seen in history books. His dark
clothing appeared as white as an angel's robes.

This man, she reminded herself, was no angel. She gave
him a long look.

While he appeared unharmed, he held his eyes shut tight,
his head slightly bowed. He seemed as if he were caught in
prayer rather than as the lone survivor of a recent fall through
the roof.

Cleo inched nearer, sidestepping the debris to stand at the
end of the iron bed. The ornate metal felt cold beneath her
fingers.

"Monsieur Breaux?"

He neither spoke nor moved. If she could move closer, she
might be able to see if he still breathed.

"Sir? Are you harmed?"

Silence. Gripping the cold metal of the bed, she leaned a
notch forward to nudge his oversized booted foot. Nothing.

Cleo's heart sunk, and tears stung her eyes. She'd really done
it this time.

As a young girl, she watched a baby bird fall from its nest
and land, seemingly unharmed, outside the parlor window.
When she rushed to its aid, she found the tiny creature
sitting as if it hadn't a care in the world. Only when she

picked it up to return it to its nest did she realize the precious baby sparrow was dead.

Theophile Breaux could have suffered the same fate. She suppressed a groan. Why hadn't she gone straight home?

If the carpenter did not survive the fall, it would be her fault. After all, if she hadn't allowed her curiosity to get the better of her, she would have gone straight home and not stopped at the cabin. Had she not stopped, she and the carpenter wouldn't have exchanged words, and he wouldn't have fallen through the roof.

It all seemed so. . .preventable. If only she could tame her persistent curiosity.

What a can of worms she'd opened by asking the Lord to help take care of the problem. First the giant snake and now this. While she fully expected to bear the cost of her improvement, she never expected someone else might be hurt along the way.

Cleo moved to the side of the bed, kicking a rather large piece of the roof out of her way. Slowly, she knelt, then peered up at the Breaux fellow's face. Traces of blood glistened from a tiny cut just beneath the fringe of dark lashes on his right eye, but he seemed otherwise unharmed.

"If you can hear me, sir, please say something." Still no sign of life.

Taking a deep breath, she bowed her head and began to pray. "Father, I really did it this time. I killed a man, or at least I hurt him badly. Lord, he didn't deserve this. He was helping us to build a school and doing a good work so the children could learn and, well, You know my part in things. I probably don't have the right to ask but—"

The mattress shuddered slightly. She paused to open her eyes and stare up at the carpenter once more. Still no sign that either Theophile Breaux or the Lord had heard her prayers.

Dropping her chin again, she continued her plea. "If You are listening, please forgive me and heal Monsieur Breaux. He might be a bit cranky, but he is one of Your children and should have a long and happy life instead of having it end just because I fooled around and got in the way. I'm the one who should pay the price for my curious nature, not he."

"Amen!"

The carpenter's chuckle seemed to shake the very floor Cleo knelt on. She jumped and nearly fell backward. As she caught herself with her elbows, she looked up to see the smiling face of Theophile Breaux.

"Well, of all the nerve." Cleo scrambled to her feet, her heart racing, and shook off as much of the dust as her trembling hands would allow.

"I'm sorry, but I am still very much alive." He dabbed gingerly at the cut beneath his eye. "Although I must say, if ever I need someone to write my eulogy, it will be you."

Realization dawned, and her eyes narrowed. "You were fine all along."

He shrugged and, for a moment, had the decency to look almost contrite. "I'm afraid so. Other than a little dust in my mouth and a few bruises in places I can't show you, I think I'll live. You look disappointed."

She opened her mouth to speak but coughed on some of that very same dust herself. When she recovered, she found the words had gone. All she could do was stand and stare at the spectacle before her.

The most irritating man on the planet had just made a total and complete fool of her. Worse, she had helped him to do it by being so. . .what? Naive? Maybe. Nosey. She groaned. Yes.

Still, he should have been a gentleman and spoken up before she bared her heart before the Lord. Even a heathen would have done that, and she knew Theophile Breaux to be a churchgoing man. Why, his granddaddy had been a preacher and his mama a preacher's daughter.

Oh, how he seemed to be enjoying her discomfort. He'd twisted that mouth of his into a grin that would have made him awfully handsome had he not been behaving just plain awful.

"I'm just sorry I had to go and laugh so soon." He shifted positions, and the old mattress creaked in protest. "I could have listened to your prayers all day."

"Heathen." There, she said it.

"Makes a man feel appreciated when a woman praises him to the Lord like that." He punctuated the statement with a wink. "I had no idea you held me in such high regard. You keep your secrets well, little girl."

How dare the man actually pull such a prank at her expense? She climbed to her feet and kicked a shingle out of her way. "You, sir, are the most despicable, dastardly man I have ever met. I do not care to linger in your presence."

He swung his long legs over the side and shook his head. Fine particles of debris rained down around him, dancing in the sunlight as they swirled and landed. "My, how your tone has changed. Am I a better man in death than in life, Mademoiselle Trahan? If so, I'd gladly die to hear you sing my praises again."

Hands on her hips, she fought her rising temper. "If I weren't a lady, Monsieur Breaux, why, I just might answer that question."

Leaning his elbows on his knees, the carpenter rested his head in his hands. "Seeing as how I've got a roof to repair, why don't we just skip the part about you being a lady and get right to it? Speak your mind. Answer the question. How *do* you feel about me? Tell me."

Oh, how she wanted to. She opened her mouth and tried. Unfortunately, all of Tante Flo's words about proper behavior came flooding back at once. The only thing she could do was turn and walk away.

"It's been a real joy, Mademoiselle Trahan." The mattress creaked once more. "Do come and see me again soon, eh?"

She paused in the doorway to turn and face him. To her surprise, he stood mere inches away, looming over her with a broad grin.

"Change your mind about running off?"

She tilted her head to stare into his eyes. "It was the schoolhouse I came to see, sir, not you, so don't flatter yourself by thinking otherwise."

This time when she made the decision to turn and flee, she did not look back or pause. Pressing past the shadows, she emerged into the bright sunshine of the porch without slowing down to allow her eyes to adjust. In the process, she ran into the porch post. A sharp jab of pain radiated up from her elbow, but thankfully, the Breaux fellow hadn't emerged from the cabin to see her near humiliation.

"You'll be back," he called from near the door. "You've already proven that you can't stay away from me."

"Humph," was the most proper answer she dared give as she stormed across the porch, heedless of the delicate condition of the boards. "Just see how I can stay away. I won't miss you a bit, that's for sure."

"Oh yes, you will," he called. "You'll miss me so bad you won't be able to stand it."

"If I do, I'll go visit the neighbor's donkey."

Oh, she'd have to apologize to the Lord for that comment. *And maybe to the carpenter, as well.*

Never.

Head held high, she forced herself not to pick up her skirts and run. His laughter chased her across the clearing.

As she stepped into the thicket, she took one last quick look over her shoulder. There stood Theophile Breaux on the porch, covered in dust and leaning against the rail with something brown hanging from the crook of his arm.

He raised a hand to wave, shaking the object as he stepped toward the edge of the porch. She ignored him and picked up her pace.

Cleo had almost reached home when she realized what the carpenter held. Her egg basket.

ða

Theo watched the Trahan woman storm off and tried to muster up some measure of irritation. After all, she'd practically caused him to kill himself and ruined three days of backbreaking work in the process.

Somehow as the swirl of yellow skirts disappeared into the thicket, he knew that trying to work up anger at Clothilde Trahan was a wasted effort. She still vexed him greatly, but the thought of making her so mad that he never saw her again didn't set well.

He placed the egg basket on the porch rail and stared at it. The new copy of *Godey's Ladies Book* it held was probably meant for Flo. He'd seen her reading a dog-eared copy just the day before yesterday and thought to buy her a new one the next time he went to town. The penny candy had to belong to Joe. As long as he'd known the man, Joe Trahan had always had a sweet of some sort in his pocket.

Returning these items along with the basket would be the neighborly thing to do. Making Clothilde Trahan eat her words and come back for the thing, however, would be the more satisfying choice.

Knowing better than to make the decision in his current state of mind, Theo left the basket on the rail and stepped off the porch, limping slowly toward the ladder. He might be a few years shy of thirty, but his bones were going to think he'd hit the century mark by bedtime.

As he hefted the ladder back into place and reached for

his hammer, he felt his muscles complain. Surely he'd go home with bruises he hadn't come to work with. Those things happened in his line of work but rarely due to female intervention.

Again, he chuckled. The Trahan girl had left her mark and not just in the toll on his body. His mind protested, as well.

He picked up his hammer and hefted the bag of nails onto his shoulder, then reached for the nearest rung on the ladder. The bruises would heal. Thoughts of Clothilde Trahan, however, promised to stay with him much longer.

eight

As the sun sank toward the tree line, Theo's conscience began to bother him more than the ache in his bones. Clothilde Trahan had most likely arrived home and been asked to explain how she came to return without the items she went to town for.

He should put the girl out of her misery and just take the basket to her. Joe had probably run out of candy by now, and Flo surely had nothing new to read. There was no sense in the two of them paying the price for their niece's silliness.

Yes, that's what he ought to do. Just a quick trip to the Trahan place, and he'd be on his way. Leaning against the porch rail, he tried to come up with a good reason why he shouldn't.

In short order, he decided there were any number of reasons for going straight home now that the dinner hour was coming soon, not the least of which that his mama had promised a big mess of shrimp étouffée and hush puppies for supper. He did love fresh-caught shrimp cooked up over rice, and his mama's cornmeal, green onion, and spice concoction made for the best hush puppies in south Louisiana.

His stomach growled at the thought. Yes, indeed, forgetting all about today and heading for a meal made for a hard-working bayou man was just the thing to end the day better than it started.

Still, there was the matter of the basket.

Scanning the horizon, he almost hoped he might see a flash of yellow that would tell him the girl was at her games again—spying from the thicket until he left so she could sneak up and fetch the lost basket. That would certainly get him off the hook, and he could go home with an empty stomach and a clear conscience. Unfortunately, no sign of anyone, male or female, greeted him.

Theo sighed and shoved the hammer into his belt as he turned his attention back to the work at hand. He'd done a fair job of patching the Breaux-sized hole in the roof and weathering it in. Tomorrow he'd begin the tedious process of lining up the shingles and hammering them in place—again.

This time he would use twice the number of nails to make the roof stronger, not that he planned to take another dive through the thing. Of course, with Clothilde Trahan on the loose, a man never knew.

Anything could happen.

Theo wiped his brow and looked off toward the west. Dark clouds had been gathering all afternoon and now rode in great gray clumps along the horizon. Their fat bodies stretched as far as the eye could see, covering the sun and leaving the earthy scent of rain in the air.

Unless he missed his guess, the night would be a stormy one. At least the cabin's front room would stay dry.

He thought of the abandoned iron bed and the feather mattress upon which he'd landed. *Someday if I marry up with that girl, I'll have to have that bedstead for our home.*

Theo nearly fell off the ladder. Where in the world had that come from?

Climbing down with care, he decided he must have hit his head on his way through the roof earlier. Nothing could be further from possible than for him to marry up with *any* bayou girl, least of all that one.

He'd wed himself to that donkey she'd told him about before he'd shackle himself to her.

For just a moment, he put aside his plans and allowed himself to wonder what it would be like to wake up next to the fiery beauty every morning until the Lord took him home. On first consideration, the idea did have some appeal, at least in the abstract.

He chuckled. Life might be entertaining, but it would never be boring. With his luck, they'd end up with a dozen daughters just like her. Now *that* was a sobering thought.

No, surely the Lord had better things for him than a trip down the aisle with a certain hardheaded busybody, even if she was the prettiest thing he ever laid eyes on. Mama told him God only held the best for each of His children, and in Theo's estimation, the best had to be something other than a life spent never knowing when he'd fall through the next roof.

Besides, he still had roads to travel and adventures to live. There was plenty of time for him to settle down someday.

Life as a married man could start after he'd seen the world— starting with Canada. He'd get there before the first snow fell and stay through the spring. After that, who knew? Alaska maybe, or perhaps he'd just hop a ship to parts unknown.

He'd always wanted to see the world. No better time than the present.

But first he had a mess of shrimp and hush puppies to eat, and if he didn't get home on time, there'd be nothing left but the crumbs.

That decided, Theo left the basket on the porch rail and headed for home. If she wanted it, she'd find it.

He got close enough to the home place to smell the shrimp frying before he turned around and headed back to the cabin to fetch the basket off the porch rail. The Lord might be willing to let Theo see the world, but it seemed as though He was telling him he needed to clear up a bit of business with Clothilde Trahan first.

Stomping his way to the Trahan place under protest, Theo clutched the basket in his hand. As he neared Joe's home, the first fat drops of rain hit him square on the head.

"Great," he grumbled as he stopped to pull the magazine from the basket and slide it beneath his shirt.

The candy fit easily into his pants pocket. Basket empty and Trahan treasures secured, Theo set back on his way as the rain began to come down in earnest.

He arrived at the Trahans' front door, soaked to the skin and starved. As he knocked, he smelled the unmistakable scent of shrimp étouffée. His stomach groaned, and so did he.

Why the Lord seemed to be picking on him today was beyond understanding.

A thought occurred. He could leave the basket right here and take off for home without any member of the Trahan family knowing he stood on their porch. He removed the slightly damp *Godey's Ladies Book* from beneath his shirt and placed it in the basket, then dumped the penny candies in after it.

Now to find a place to leave the basket where it wouldn't get wet. The porch rail was out of the question as the rain poured down upon it. A swing sat at the far end of the porch, but it might be days before someone thought to look all the way down there.

"Come on in here out of the weather."

Theo jumped and nearly sent the basket and its contents flying across the porch. He gathered his wits and turned to see Flo standing at the door, an apron tied around her waist and a dish towel thrown over one shoulder.

"Well, actually I just brought—"

"Is that Theo Breaux?" Joe Trahan pressed past his wife to shake Theo's hand. "How's it going, boy? You come by to share supper with us?"

He thrust the basket in Joe's direction. Rather than take it, Joe stared at the item as if he'd never seen it, then turned his gaze on Theo.

"Did my niece know you'd be visiting tonight?"

"No, I don't think so," he said, although it was just a guess.

Flo looped her hand around the basket's handle and smiled. "Well, thank you for bringing this by, Theo. Especially in this weather. I'm so pleased to have something new to read. And Joe, isn't it nice that Theo would go to all this trouble to bring your penny candy by tonight?"

Relief flooded Theo's aching bones. "It was no trouble, really."

Joe took a step toward Theo and grasped him by the elbow. "Flo, set another place at the table. Theo and I'll be in just as soon as we talk some business."

Theo made a weak attempt to protest, but Flo had already disappeared inside. He turned his attention to Joe. Maybe he could talk his way out of staying. Surely Joe Trahan wouldn't hold a man to a dinner invitation he didn't want to accept.

"I appreciate the offer," Theo said, "but I really ought to get on home."

Joe tightened his grip on Theo's elbow past the point where it felt neighborly. Theo looked down into the older Cajun's eyes and saw something that surprised him.

The man looked positively angry.

"I'm glad you stopped by, young man." He motioned to the swing on the far end of the porch. "Go sit down. I was speaking the truth when I told Flo you and I had some business to discuss. If you hadn't had the decency to show up at my front door tonight, I would have been at yours before bedtime."

From the look on Joe's face and the urgency in his words, there was something big going on down at the schoolhouse. The last thing Theo needed was to try and make sense of another set of building plans.

It was hard enough to make out the chicken scratching Joe wrote on the pages he regularly gave Theo. Generally Theo would smile and do the best he could, then take the papers home for his brother Alphonse to decipher. Tonight of all nights he just didn't have the strength to deal with it.

"Honestly, sir, it's been a long day," he said with the best smile he could muster. "How about I come a little early for coffee in the morning? We can talk all you want then, eh?"

Joe leveled a hard stare in Theo's direction. "After I finish with you, I'm not sure you and I will be having coffee in the mornings anymore."

nine

Cleo drew back from the window and sucked in a deep breath. Whatever happened between Uncle Joe and the Breaux fellow, neither seemed to be happy about it. She could certainly sympathize. His arrival on their doorstep hadn't exactly filled her with joy, either.

At least he'd returned the basket.

"Clothilde Trahan, are you spying again?" Tante Flo stood at the parlor door with a frown and a dish towel. She held the basket in the crook of her elbow. "I thought you learned your lesson when that boy out there fell through the roof this afternoon."

Cleo had told her aunt the whole story when she arrived home earlier that afternoon, even backtracking to describe the previous incident with the snake. Of course, telling Tante Flo had been easy compared to worrying about delivering the news to Uncle Joe that her snooping had almost ended in disaster—twice.

"I saw the lightning and wondered if we had a storm coming." Cleo released the hem of the starched cotton curtain. "I didn't know we had company."

Her aunt set the basket on the sideboard. "So you weren't expecting him?"

"No."

But *had* she expected him? Cleo wasn't sure how to answer.

A gentleman would have saved her the trip and the explanations. A man like she figured Theophile Breaux to be would have waited to gloat when she finally returned to the cabin to claim it.

"I thought I might find Uncle Joe alone and speak to him about what happened this afternoon before we sat down to supper. Do you think he spied me coming up the road this afternoon?"

"All I know's if he did, he never said anything to me." Tante Flo shrugged. "But then he's been busy all day doing this and that. Until he came in to wash up for supper, I hadn't seen hide nor hair of him since lunchtime."

"I just hope he was too busy to notice." Cleo looked away. "If he saw me before I had a chance to brush the pine needles out of my hair, he probably thought the same thing you did."

Tante Flo's frown tilted into a smile as her fingers worried with the end of the dish towel. "What else is a mother to think when her girl comes home from town covered in dust and her hair all in a mess? And the basket, well, I asked myself why wasn't it with her?"

"Yes, I know," she said softly. "I'm sorry."

"I'm not your real mama, but I sure feel like it, and I don't keep my mouth shut at times like that."

Stepping away from the window, Cleo embraced her aunt. "I'm so glad you feel that way. I wonder if you guessed what a trouble I'd be."

"Trouble? Nonsense. Why this old house has become a home since you came to live in it."

Cleo shook her head. "That's very kind, but I doubt you expected you would end up with someone so. . .well. . . curious."

"Oh, child, you're so like your mama at her age. So full of life and smart. Why, that girl could outthink just about anybody, then charm them into not caring. And curious? Well, you've not seen curiosity until you've seen Marie." Tante Flo held Cleo at arm's length and shook her head. "I miss her so, but it's like a little bit of Marie still lives on in you. You've been a blessing."

Cleo gave her a sideways look. "Even when I'm a busybody?"

Her aunt pretended to study the question with great concern. She chuckled. "When you put it that way, well. . ."

A movement outside the window reflected in the pier glass over the sideboard caught Cleo's attention. It was Uncle Joe, and he seemed to be pacing. The murmur of his deep voice rattled the windowpane, but the words were undecipherable. The tone, however, sounded decidedly angry.

"Oh dear," Tante Flo said softly. Her gaze met Cleo's. "I think we ought to walk ourselves to the other side of the house and see to supper. You stir the étouffée, and I'll mix up the hush puppies."

Cleo snatched the basket and followed her aunt out of the parlor. An ache had begun in the pit of her stomach. No matter how good Tante Flo's cooking was, she doubted she'd be partaking tonight.

❧

"Monsieur Trahan, if you'll just calm down, I'm sure we—"

"Calm down?" Joe stopped his pacing and stood at the far end of the porch, hands on hips. "Calm down?"

Planting his feet firmly on the porch boards, Theo stood. "Sir, I think there's been some misunderstanding here. I'm not sure what I've done to set you off but—"

"Sit down!"

Although he was the bigger of the pair and younger than Joe by a decade and a half, Theo did as he was told.

Joe began to make a path across the porch again, passing the window where Theo had spied Clothilde standing moments ago. She was gone now, or at least she had the good sense to observe from a less visible spot.

Theo turned his attention away from the house and off toward the horizon. The rain seemed to be coming in fits and starts, blowing hard, then tapering off. Right now, there was nothing but a light drizzle falling from the eaves—a good time to make a run for home.

Except that his respect for Joe Trahan wouldn't let him move from the porch until he'd heard what Joe had to say. Judging from the way the man had taken up his pacing once more, he might be there awhile.

While he had no idea what had set Joe off, he knew better than to try and say anything to further aggravate him. One thing he knew for sure: Bringing the basket back was a mistake.

Theo leaned back and heard the chains protest and clank. His stomach growled, joining the chorus of noises. Off in the distance, a flash of lightning zigzagged through the evening sky. The fresh smell of rain teased his nose and warned him that the lull in the weather soon would end.

He'd most likely be going home tonight hungry and wet.

Finally Joe stopped short and grabbed a straight-backed chair and shoved it near the swing. He turned the chair backward and settled on the seat, resting his arms on the back. Eyes narrowed, he stared at Theo as if he expected Theo to know what had brought on his fit of anger.

"Anything you want to tell me, boy?" He shifted positions slightly but never broke his stare. "Because in my experience, a man owns up to his misdeeds up front. Now am I mistaken about judging you as a man?"

What in the world is Joe Trahan talking about?

"Sir, I'm not sure how to answer that. Is there something in particular we're talking about? Something I've done that's got you riled up?" A thought dawned, and along with it a possible explanation for Joe's anger. "Have you been talking to Alphonse?"

The older man looked puzzled. "What does your brother have to do with this?"

"Well, I just thought that maybe he. . .that is, considering I am supposed to be able to. . ." As Joe's confusion became more apparent, Theo stopped talking altogether. "Never mind."

Perhaps that secret was still safe. If so, then what was the trouble?

Joe made a slashing motion through the damp air with his hand. "Let's get right to it, young man. You got a problem with plain talk?"

Theo sat up a little straighter and squared his shoulders. "No, sir. In fact, I prefer it."

"Good." Joe grabbed the back of the chair with both hands, turning his knuckles white. He lowered his gaze and seemed to be studying the floor. "This isn't a conversation I ever hoped to have."

Theo's stomach complained again, and a gust of wind blew cold raindrops down his back. "Whatever it is, I'd appreciate if you'd get on with that plain talk."

Joe nodded and looked up. "That I will." He let out a long breath. "This is in regard to my niece, Clothilde."

Good. Finally a topic he could warm to.

Joe must have heard his pesky niece was snooping around the cabin today. *Serves her right to suffer her uncle's ire.* The only puzzle was why Joe seemed to be taking out a share of that irritation on him.

He pointed his finger at Theo. "Unless you can give me a good reason why my niece came home this afternoon with her clothes in a mess and her hair full of dust and pine needles, the next man you'll be talking plain with is going to be the reverend."

Theo opened his mouth to say something—anything—in his defense. Instead of allowing him to speak the words that would get him out of this mess, his mouth went dry and refused to work.

"Say something, Theophile Breaux, before I get my shotgun and loosen your jaw."

"Go ahead and tell him, young man."

He looked past Joe to where Clothilde's aunt stood at the front door. Again he failed to force words of innocence from his mouth.

She strolled across the porch to rest her hand on her husband's shoulder. "Joe, the funniest thing happened today out at the cabin." Meeting Theo's gaze, she nodded. "Don't be afraid to tell him about that hole in the roof my niece caused you to make. I got a good laugh out of the story when Cleo told me this afternoon."

Theo nodded. "Yes, well, you see, I was patching the roof over on the north side."

"That weak spot over the parlor?" Joe asked.

"Oui." Theo paused to swallow hard, praying the words wouldn't leave him again. "I was leaning over to make sure those nails were in straight when I spied a flash of yellow over to the east in the thicket."

"Clothilde," Joe said under his breath.

"Yes, sir, it was. I figured her for just hiding out and watching a spell, but she surprised me."

"I whistled." Clothilde stood at the door, leaning against the frame. "Well, I *did*," she said when her aunt and uncle turned to face her.

"So you didn't know she was underfoot?" Joe asked.

"No, sir. Before I knew what happened, there she stood at the bottom of the ladder, talking to me as if I'd seen her walk up." He continued to stare past the Trahans to their niece, eyes narrowed. "Which I *didn't*."

"I made plenty of noise. I didn't want him to think I was spying." She stared right back at him. "I thought you heard me."

"I was hammering." While he *had* heard whistling, he had no recollection of thinking it might be the Trahan girl.

Clothilde toyed with the end of her braid. "Not constantly."

"Enough for any normal person to know a man was working." Theo felt his blood begin to boil. "Last thing I expected was for you to change your mind about never seeing me again and pay me a visit while you were out on your stroll."

"I wasn't out for a stroll. I went to town on an errand."

"Which you failed to complete until I brought the basket back." Theo stood. "For all the grief it's caused me, I should have waited for you to come and get the stupid basket."

Joe rose and pushed the chair away. "I believe I've heard enough." He took his wife by the hand. "Why I thought there were shenanigans between these two is beyond me. I don't think I've ever met a more mismatched pair."

Flo offered a smile before she headed for the door. Joe disappeared inside, leaving Theo alone with Clothilde Trahan. At that moment, he decided taking his chances with the storm brewing on the other side of the porch rail was preferable to staying and risking another five minutes with the female tornado.

"Theo," Joe called. "Come on in here and get yourself some supper. I can hear your stomach growling from here."

Theo looked up at Clothilde. The object of his thoughts stood arrow straight with her arms crossed and her eyes narrowed. He felt about as welcome as that big cottonmouth.

"*Merci beaucoup,* sir, but I believe I'll just go on home."

Joe appeared in the doorway and pointed at Clothilde. "Get on in there and set this young man a plate. It's the least you can do, considering you nearly killed him this afternoon." As Cleo pressed past to disappear inside, Joe turned his attention to Theo. "Good thing my mother's bed never got moved out of the parlor after she passed on."

"You knew I fell through the roof?"

"Boy, that much was obvious." Joe shook his head. "What I *didn't* know was what part my niece played in the whole mess and where she was when you landed on the mattress." He paused. "Or where she ended up afterward."

Theo let out a pent-up breath and smiled. "I'm sure you can see you have nothing to worry about when it comes to your niece and me."

The older man gave him a level stare. "I see nothing of the sort. Watch yourself with that girl, or next time your fall won't be off a ladder."

⤫

Only later, across the kitchen table from Clothilde Trahan, after spending several hours sharing a meal and conversation, did Theo realize what her uncle had meant. By then, it was too late.

He'd fallen hard for Clothilde Trahan—and this time it had nothing to do with a hole in the roof.

The realization hit him somewhere between the shrimp étouffée and hush puppies and the sweet cake *gateau de sirop*. He'd been minding his own business, sipping chicory coffee and listening to Joe and his wife finish each other's sentences and laugh at each other's silly jokes, when he felt the wall around his heart begin to crack.

I want what they have. He suppressed a groan as he snuck a peek across the table at Clothilde Trahan. *And I want it with her.*

She smiled, first at her aunt and uncle and then at him. He tried and failed to return the gesture.

Lord, please take this feeling away. You and I have a deal, and it doesn't include Clothilde Trahan.

Until He did, Theo knew he'd just have to stay out of her way.

ten

Cleo swiped at the bottom of Uncle Joe's coffee cup with the dish towel, then set it on the drain board to dry. Once again, Cleo had only one cup to wash. Nearly a week had passed since Uncle Joe had had company in the morning for coffee.

And by company, she meant Theophile Breaux.

No sight of the Breaux fellow graced the front porch, nor did he come around on Sunday after church to talk to Uncle Joe. The only time Cleo had seen Theophile Breaux had been Sunday morning during services and then only from a distance. Rather than sit with his family in their usual third pew from the front, the carpenter chose to slip in the side door as the opening hymn began and sneak out the same way when the last strains of the hymn of invitation ended.

His behavior seemed even stranger since they'd spent such a lovely evening with her aunt and uncle—after the incident on the porch, that is. Cleo had actually begun to think that Theophile Breaux just might be a nice man.

The ruffled curtain swayed in the stiff, north wind, winter's last dance before spring dawned on the bayou. Cleo suppressed a chill and inhaled the sweet scent of Easter lilies. She and Tante Flo spent hours babying the beautiful blossoms and had been rewarded with a bountiful crop.

They'd bloomed early, and as long as a freeze didn't come along before Easter Sunday, there would be plenty of fragrant white blossoms to decorate the altar at church. Before spring ended and the heat of summer set in, she would have to think about separating them out and creating a new bed with what they didn't give to neighbors and friends. Come winter, the process of growing the lilies would begin all over again.

Cleo wiped her hands, then tossed the dish towel over the drying rack. One chore down. What to do next?

She could polish the silver, but her aunt usually shared that job with her. Good conversation and frequent laughter often took place over the shiny pile of forks and spoons.

Tante Flo had gone to take a mess of freshly fried chicken to the Landry family down the bayou a ways. They had a new baby, born just last Wednesday.

Although Tante Flo claimed dropping off a meal was the neighborly thing to do, she always seemed to be most eager to visit the new mothers. Cleo suspected it might have something to do with the babies her aunt loved so much.

"She should have been a mama many times over. Too bad all she got was nosey old me." Cleo chuckled and reached for the broom. "I hope I do better than that."

As she swept the cobwebs out of the corners, she allowed her mind to drift to a time and place far in the future where she had a home of her own and a passel of children. In her mind, a brown-eyed son smiled up at her while a daughter with dark curls crawled at her feet. She pressed forward in time until she could imagine children of various sizes running and playing on the green lawn. Finally, a pair of twins—one a girl and the other a boy—chased butterflies past thick patches of Easter lilies.

"I'll have a boy first and name him Ernest. The second, of course, will be a girl with dark hair like her mama. I'll call her Angeline."

She closed her eyes and smiled. The broom became her partner in an imaginary dance watched by the children she'd have someday.

Swaying to music only she could hear, she pictured her groom.

And saw Theophile Breaux.

Cleo's eyes flew open, and she dropped the broom. "Oh my," she said under her breath. "That's odd."

As she reached for the broom, a clanging sound made her jump. The mail boat.

Dropping the broom in the middle of the kitchen floor, she raced out the back door and headed for the little dock on the bayou. The arrival of a mail boat was rare—only once a month if that often—so the warning bell only had to be sounded once. Before the boat could dock, Cleo stood waiting for whatever the postman brought.

"Mademoiselle Trahan?"

"*Oui. C'est moi.*"

As the portly, gray-haired gentleman dug down into a seemingly bottomless leather pouch marked UNITED STATES MAIL, Cleo tried not to fidget. Several times he examined letters or parcels through his thick spectacles, only to drop them back into the pouch. She found her patience nearly at an end when the fellow triumphantly pulled out a fistful of letters and thrust them toward her.

"*Merci beaucoup, monsieur.*" She gathered the letters in her apron and raced toward the house.

"You're welcome," he called as he stepped back into the mail boat.

Waiting until she reached the kitchen to look at the letters was near to impossible, but somehow Cleo managed. When she finally reached the kitchen, she lifted the hem of her apron and let the papers spill onto the table.

Two notes from relatives and a postcard from her friend Margie covered a third envelope with a familiar return address: New Orleans.

Cleo lifted the letter from the pile and stared at the writing. Beneath the name of the college was the unmistakable handwriting—and name—of Uncle Joe's friend.

She dropped the letter onto the stack and took a step

back. What to do? Waiting until Uncle Joe returned from his meeting with the reverend occurred to her, but only for a moment. Those meetings could take half the afternoon. And wait for Tante Flo? Well, that could mean she might not see the contents of the letter until after supper.

Inching forward, Cleo picked up the letter with her thumb and forefinger and held it to the stream of sunlight spilling through the kitchen window. Only the slightest outline of decidedly male handwriting appeared.

She sighed. In order to read the letter, she must open it.

Cleo dropped the letter into her pocket and made a neat stack of the remaining mail. Rather than read the letter immediately, she decided to wait in hopes that Uncle Joe might cut his visit short and return soon.

Actually, she hoped he didn't cut his visit short, but somehow delaying her plan to open the letter seemed better than doing it immediately. Retrieving the broom, she finished the job of sweeping out the kitchen, then patted her apron pocket. The letter felt stiff beneath the soft fabric.

With another glance out the kitchen window to ensure neither her aunt nor her uncle approached, Cleo slipped upstairs to her bedroom. She made short order of opening the letter. Actually reading it, however, took a bit longer.

First she had to close her eyes, and then she decided to pray. When she opened her eyes, she grasped the envelope and wedged it open. Barely breathing, she pulled the letter out and unfolded it.

Her eyes scanned the opening lines:

Dearest Joe,
 It is with great pleasure that I received your letter of 4 March. For that reason, I felt a quick response was in order. Thus, I held the postman in waiting until I could write a brief note of. . .

The lines of handwriting on the page began to shake. When she realized it was her hands that quivered, she released the paper and let it fall to the coverlet.

"Maybe I don't want to know this." Cleo held her breath, then let it out slowly. "It might be bad news."

She stared down at the letter. *Just one more sentence, maybe two. If the news is bad, I'll reseal the letter and return it to the stack.*

Taking care to lift the letter by the corner, she leaned back against the wall and tucked her feet beneath her. Another deep breath, and she began to read again:

. . .a brief note of delight that you are committed to the education of the children in Latagnier. You and I have long believed local schools are sorely needed in remote areas of Louisiana, and I am most interested in helping you to fill the position of teacher that the new school will require.

Cleo smiled. "Well, nothing terrible yet. He's happy we're going to have a school, but who wouldn't be? And of course he's interested in filling the position. He works at a teachers' college."

With renewed hope, she went back to her reading:

And thus, in the spirit of friendship, I will be more than happy to come to your assistance by providing you with the name of a suitable candidate. In fact, I have taken the liberty of speaking to a colleague of mine who happened to be in my office at the time your letter was delivered. This colleague, a learned woman by the name of Ellen Granville, would be most pleased to take on the education of the local children, and she is. . .

"No," Cleo whispered. "It can't be."

Once again, she let the paper fall. This time it sailed past the coverlet and lodged between the washbasin and the wall. She fell back against the pillows and tried not to cry. Failing that, she let the tears flow and closed her eyes.

When she opened her eyes once more, the sun slanted through her windows, waking Cleo from what was a brief but fitful sleep. She blinked hard, then shook her head to dislodge the cobwebs from her brain. Was it morning?

She looked out the window at the position of the sun. Hardly morning, it seemed more like midafternoon. Cleo rose and washed her face in the basin, then patted it dry. As she returned the towel to its place, she noticed the slip of paper at her feet.

The letter.

Bending to retrieve it, she allowed the page to fall open. As she reread the words her uncle's friend had penned, she noticed she hadn't read the entire text of the letter.

> *. . .and she is pleased to state that pending your favorable response, she will arrive in Latagnier at summer's end.*

"At summer's end." Cleo whispered the words, then repeated them, rolling the sounds over on her tongue as she enunciated each syllable with care.

What lovely words they were. Words that bought her an entire summer's worth of time to convince Uncle Joe that she should be the teacher, not some woman named Ellen Granville whose only credentials were a college education and a letter of recommendation from Uncle Joe's friend.

Cleo giggled. So much could happen between now and summer's end. After all, March was on its way out, and April dawned in two days. In five months' time, Cleo fully expected to have the children of Latagnier on their way to a well-rounded education and to have her uncle convinced that another teacher was unnecessary.

Folding the page back into its original shape and inserting it in the envelope, she tucked it into her pocket and pinched her cheeks to heighten the color. With five months until her deadline, she would definitely need a partner to see it to completion.

As she passed the kitchen table, she gave passing thought to replacing the letter in the pile of mail. Instead, she decided to own up to reading the letter in person rather than risk Uncle Joe or Tante Flo finding the evidence before she returned.

Crossing the lawn, she veered toward the path leading along the bayou, then struck out for the far end of the property where the little cabin—and her future—awaited. It wasn't until she neared the building site that she began to have second thoughts.

What if the carpenter went to her uncle with the news that she'd been meddling? Worse, what if she caught him by surprise again and caused him to. . .well, she just wouldn't think on that. This time she'd call his name from the time she stepped out of the thicket until she neared the cabin. Until he responded, she'd just keep calling.

This decided, she picked up her pace, stepping carefully through the thicket lest the big cottonmouth left any friends or family behind. The thought of asking the carpenter for help made meeting a snake seem positively fun.

Signs of progress greeted her as she neared the cabin. The roof seemed to have been patched, and the porch no longer held rotten boards on its newly painted floor. Even the handrails seemed to stand straighter, although they did not yet wear a new coat of paint.

Cleo peered into the parlor window. The mess she'd encountered upon her last trip here had been replaced by a room swept clean of wood and dust. Grandma's bed still stood in the center of the room, but it had been stripped of its mattress, which now sat rolled up in the corner.

Was it her imagination or perhaps a trick of the light? Rather than wearing the signs of age, the old iron bed seemed to have been polished to a bright shine.

"Strange."

She walked to the front door and pushed on it, smiling when it gave way. "Monsieur Breaux," she called.

No answer.

Cleo stepped inside and looked around. This part had also been cleared away, and the wall that formerly divided the space had been removed. Marks on another wall showed where the carpenter planned to create space for a new door.

To her right, an area perfect for rows of students to sit greeted her. On her left, she saw a place for the old desk from Uncle Joe's attic. The center had been left open, a grand space despite its tiny proportions.

Wrapping her arms around herself, Cleo tried to imagine what the room would be like once it had been filled with children. With the windows open to the breeze off the bayou and the cobwebs gone, this would be a fit schoolroom.

The carpenter had outdone himself.

"Merci beaucoup, Lord," she whispered as she made her way to the door and emerged into the bright sunshine.

She stepped carefully off the porch and called the Breaux fellow's name once more. Still no answer.

Rounding the corner, she spied Theophile Breaux standing beside a pile of lumber, a saw in one hand. When she waved, he seemed to ignore her. As she called his name, he shook his head.

"Go on home," came the gruff response.

"I'd like a word with you." She ignored his frown to offer a smile. "Please," she added. "I won't take up much time. I promise."

"You already have," he said as he pressed past her to head for the cabin, then disappeared around the corner.

eleven

Theo tempered his anger as he stomped across the porch. His first inclination was to give the heavy front door a swift kick or, better yet, to send it swinging so hard it flew off the hinges.

But slamming the door and causing something he had repaired to break again wouldn't serve any good. Given his frustration level, it sure would feel dandy about now, however.

Still, he'd be the one who would have to fix it, and extra repairs meant extra time in Latagnier. The last thing he needed was more time in this town.

More time in close proximity to Clothilde Trahan.

"Last thing I need," he grumbled.

Theo stomped inside, leaving the front door standing open. He didn't dare touch it for fear he'd go against his good intentions and close the thing so hard he'd bust out the frame and half the front wall.

A swirl of blue caught his attention outside. He stopped short. Clothilde Trahan still stood beside the woodpile, her skirts swaying in the fresh breeze. While he watched, the wind picked up her waist-length braid, then let it drop once more. All the while, she seemed to be staring at a point opposite the house.

Theo stepped back when she directed her attention toward the cabin. What on earth was she doing here?

He'd certainly reminded himself and the Lord of his promise to keep his distance from her, and yet there the woman remained. From his vantage point, she seemed to be in no hurry to leave.

She pulled an envelope from her apron pocket, took out a piece of paper, and unfolded it, taking care to keep it from flying away as she turned her back to the wind. Head bowed, she studied the paper, then refolded the page, returned it to the envelope, and put it back in her pocket.

Maybe she'll understand I want nothing to do with her, and she'll go home. He stood there a moment longer in hopes of watching her disappear into the thicket, but she never moved.

Theo grumbled under his breath and set to work on the one chore that seemed appropriate to the moment—demolishing something.

With every swing of the sledgehammer, his muscles—and his heart—pulled and twisted. As each piece of wall crumbled and fell, so did his resolve, until he knew he could stand it no longer.

Listen to her.

He let the heavy tool fall to the floor and swiped at his brow. What?

The words had come to him as plain as if someone stood beside him and had whispered in his ear. He looked behind him and to the right and the left. He was alone.

Listen to her.

There. He heard it again. "Who's there?" he called.

No answer.

Then, in the depths of his heart, he realized whose voice he'd heard. Goose bumps rose on his arms.

Just listen.

Theo leaned against what was left of the wall and shook his head. He was a churchgoing man and a believer in the ever-reaching power of God, but never had the Lord spoken to him in such a clear voice.

Figured He'd be asking for the last thing Theo wanted to do.

Arguing with the Creator of the universe seemed pointless,

but obedience felt even less logical. What could that silly girl have to tell him that he didn't already know?

Plenty.

Theo straightened his back and set his jaw. If he must do as he was told, at least he could try and make one last deal.

All right, Lord, You win. If she's still out there, I'll hear her out. Remember, though, You and I made a deal, and I'm supposed to be free to head out of here whenever I wish.

He paused, thinking the Lord might answer. He didn't.

All right, then. If I have a say in things, could You see to her not being there, and we'll just call this conversation between me and her over before it starts? I'd be much obliged. I promise I'll listen just like You said next time I see her.

Once again, God was silent on the subject.

Whichever way You want it then, Father. I want what You want, or at least I'm trying to.

Adding a quick amen to his prayer, Theo set off toward the back of the cabin, where a glance out the window showed him the Lord had indeed answered his prayer.

She was gone.

No flowing blue skirts or dancing black braid greeted him. No big brown eyes or pretty face to charm him and scare the living daylights out of him all at the same time. Only the woodpile and a skinny orange cat with a bent tail and an ornery look were framed by the window.

"Well, how about that?"

Theo couldn't help it. Right there he threw back his head and laughed out loud. He chuckled like a fool, laughing so hard his side began to ache.

"Thank You, Jesus," he shouted to the rafters. "Thank You, thank You, thank You!"

As he headed back to the front of the cabin with a spring in his step, he began to whistle the closing hymn from last week's church service. It was a peppy tune, one of those songs that seeps joy all the way down to the bone and causes the toes to tap. He made it all the way to the second stanza before he picked up the sledgehammer and aimed it once more at the remnants of the wall.

Wood crumbled beneath each blow until bits and pieces of shattered timber littered the floor and decorated his clothing. While he worked, he whistled, giving thanks to God with each stroke of the sledgehammer.

The job completed, Theo paused to shake the particles from his hair and wipe his brow.

"Finally. I couldn't say a thing for all that noise," came the sweet voice behind him.

Clothilde Trahan.

Theo whirled around to see the vision in blue sitting primly on the lone chair in the room. In his astonishment, he dropped the sledgehammer. It landed with a thud on his left foot, and he howled.

"Of all the—" Theo bit his lip and stared at the menace in blue.

He looked down at his foot, as much to check the damage as to keep his gaze from meeting hers. While there seemed to be no outward damage, it hurt something awful. No, it throbbed. He'd have a hard time sleeping tonight for sure.

And it would be a long walk—or rather hobble—home.

He risked a glance and saw the girl sitting peacefully on the edge of her chair. Something about her calm expression sparked his ire.

She seemed to be enjoying herself immensely. "I'm terribly sorry. I thought you knew I was standing there."

"You know, Mademoiselle Trahan, I once had a pretty mare by the name of Stella," he said through gritted teeth. "Every time I came close to her, she would bite me." He moved a step closer to the smiling source of irritation. "When I put a saddle on her, she stomped my feet, and when I managed to ride her, she threw me every time."

Theo paused to gauge Cleo's reaction. She gave nothing of her feelings away. He closed the distance between them in three steps and stood towering over her.

"I finally figured out that every time she and I shared the same space, something bad happened to me."

He leaned down to get on eye level, being careful to favor the foot that did not ache. The Trahan woman sat very still and silent. Only her large eyes gave an indication he might be causing her some measure of upset.

"So," he said slowly, "the day came when I decided enough was enough. Do you know what I did with that mare?"

She leaned slightly back, putting some distance between them. "What?"

"I traded her to a circuit-riding preacher for a can of beans and a new hammer."

"Oh?"

"That's right. Next time I saw that preacher, he tried to return her. Said he was tired of wondering when his next bruise was coming. I gave him back his beans and hammer and sent the horse out to pasture."

"Really?"

"*Oui.*" He paused to give his message full effect. "You, Mademoiselle Trahan, remind me very much of Stella. Just like that circuit-riding preacher, I wonder where my next bruise is coming from whenever you're around."

For a moment, she seemed to be waiting for the rest of the story. Then she nodded as though understanding dawned. *"Merci."*

What in the world? He shook his head, then gave her a sideways glance. "Excuse me?"

"That Stella must have been one smart horse. She ended up getting her way after all." The woman had the audacity to grin. "I appreciate the comparison."

Cleo watched with smug satisfaction, then remorse, as the big man's handsome face turned several shades of scarlet. Of course she knew he hadn't meant to compliment her by comparing her to some ornery horse he used to own.

She should be ashamed for teasing him. If only she didn't find it so easy to spark his ire—and so much fun. Unfortunately, her behavior had done nothing to gain his cooperation in her plan.

Her plan.

Staring up into Theophile Breaux's eyes, she almost forgot her plan. *Time to make amends.*

"Monsieur Breaux, I'm terribly sorry." She rose and ducked under his watchful gaze and walked toward the window. A sweet orange cat lounged on the woodpile. She watched it swat at a butterfly and miss. "I know I've caused you much distress."

"Distress?" He repeated the word. "Now what makes you think that?"

She waved away his question with a lift of her hand. "No need to spare my feelings. I realize I tend to cause, well, disasters when I'm around you."

He said nothing, and she dared not turn to gauge his expression. Instead, she watched the cat yawn and settle in for a nap atop the woodpile, then felt for the letter in her pocket.

"I'm sorry about causing you to hurt your foot today and for all the other bruises I've inflicted." She turned around slowly. "None was intentional."

The carpenter stood in the shadows, arms crossed over his chest. His face showed no sign of emotion. "Never thought they were."

"I should get to the reason why I came here."

His lips quirked into a wry smile. "There's a reason?"

Cleo thought a moment before plunging into an explanation of her plan. "The sooner my uncle sees how well I can teach the children, the sooner he will realize he doesn't need to hire a teacher from that fancy college in New Orleans."

When Theophile offered no response, Cleo closed the distance between them to press on with her explanation. "Or maybe he will be so impressed with my abilities that he will send *me* to the college. Either way, I need your help."

He peered down at her with a look of amusement. "Why me? Surely there are other men you can torture, eh?"

"I'm going to ignore that comment, Monsieur Breaux." She took a deep breath of dusty air, then tried not to cough. "The time is limited, and I really need you to get busy finishing the schoolhouse before this happens." She pulled the letter out of her pocket and waved it under the carpenter's nose. "It came today."

Theophile took a step back and shook his head. "Wait a minute. What are you talking about?"

Unfolding the letter, she thrust it in his direction. "Here, read it for yourself."

He waved away the paper and turned to reach for the sledgehammer. "I'm too busy to be trifled with, Mademoiselle Trahan. *Allons.* Go home to your aunt and uncle."

Cleo trotted behind him as he strode into the fresh air. As he stepped off the porch, she followed, fairly running to keep up with his long, hobbled strides.

"Wait. You don't understand. You're the only one who can help me," she called, yet he kept walking.

Finally she lunged forward to grasp the carpenter by the elbow. To her surprise, he whirled around, causing her to run into him. Stunned, she reeled back and let go of the letter. It fluttered to the ground, where Theophile retrieved it.

"Here, now go home." He tried to place the letter in her hand, but she refused to take it.

"Just read the letter," she said as she tested her balance and straightened her apron. "Then maybe you'll understand why I need your help."

He carried the letter like it might burn him, barely touching the edges of the paper with his thumb and forefinger as he held it at arm's length.

The flush of scarlet anger caused earlier now reappeared on his face. His expression bore something besides anger. Was it embarrassment? Cleo studied the carpenter closely.

Eyes downcast, he placed the letter in her hand. Without a word, he tossed the sledgehammer atop the woodpile. Thankfully the orange cat had already lit out for parts unknown, for Theophile certainly hadn't so much as cast a glance in that direction before he made his throw.

"What?" she called as he strode away. "What did I do this time?"

Again she raced to catch up. "It's this letter, isn't it?"

He slowed his uneven pace but not by much. "What is it you want from me?" he asked over his shoulder as he headed for the thicket.

"I came to ask you to speed up the repairs on the cabin so I can begin teaching sooner, that's all. I want a chance to show Uncle Joe that I can do the job." She took a deep breath and darted to cut him off, coming to a halt on the path between him and the bayou. "This letter says the new teacher will be here by the end of summer. See?"

She stuck the letter under his nose and pointed to the line telling her uncle when the teacher would arrive. The carpenter stared in the direction of her finger, but curiously, his eyes did not seem to be reading, nor did he look to comprehend the information the page contained.

"Oh, no," she whispered as realization dawned. "You can't read."

twelve

"I'm so sorry," the girl called as Theo made tracks toward the bayou and the road home. "Please forgive me," followed him on the breeze.

Forgive? Forgetting was more his concern, for he never wanted to think on the events of this day again.

Never had he been so humiliated. Leave it to the Trahan girl to hit him right where it hurt, and he wasn't thinking of his sore foot. What *was* it about that woman? If she wasn't inflicting bruises on his body, she was paining his heart.

In this case, she had no idea what she'd done. If only he'd managed to hide his lack of education. Always before he'd been able to bluff his way through any situation where reading was required. Why, he'd sat at Joe Trahan's kitchen table any number of times and looked at the scribbles and lines Joe put on the page, never letting on he couldn't decipher them.

He'd always tucked the pages into his pocket and taken them home for his brother Alphonse to read, and then he'd come back to the Trahan place the next morning armed with the information contained on the pages. If Joe's snoopy little niece hadn't barged into his life, his secret would still be safe.

Now the whole town of Latagnier would know that Theophile Breaux was illiterate. Oh, he knew plenty of pretty words, and his mama made sure he used them correctly. He just couldn't make any sense of them on a page. Worse, when he opened Mama's Bible, the words made as much sense as the scratching the chickens made in the dirt.

It wasn't that he didn't want to read. He did. Unfortunately, there had been no time for book learning.

The eldest of the bunch, he'd always been called on to help Papa with the trapping or the trotlines, so schooling had been sparse through the years. Finally, when he grew two heads taller than the other students and stuck out like a sore thumb in the classroom, he gave it up altogether.

Sometimes in church he prayed that the Lord would help him make sense of the garbled letters and numbers that made up scripture and hymns. Other times he decided he was destined to go through life with other folks reading it to him.

Never, though, had he envisioned anyone besides Alphonse knowing his shortcoming. He'd always been a quick study, fast to learn and memorize and faster still to pretend he could decipher the words on paper. Papa never knew, or he'd be disappointed for sure, being as he'd nearly gone to college. The fact that the Trahan girl had been the one to figure it out stung.

"Please don't go," the object of his thoughts called. "Come back."

He debated for a half second before picking up his pace, grimacing with every step. A moment later, he entered the thicket. If he was lucky, she'd run into difficulties with that skirt and apron of hers and be unable to pass through the narrow path.

A tap on his back answered the question of his luck—not that he truly believed such a thing existed. It just seemed easier to blame luck, or the lack of it, than the Lord for his current situation.

Theo cast a glance behind him and was greeted by Clothilde's smiling face. She had a lot more stamina than he expected, especially for a girl of her small size wearing a pretty spring frock. Of course, he could outrun her if he wanted, even with the handicap of an injured foot, but somehow he knew he'd never get rid of her that way.

Better to face his nemesis here and now than to wonder when she would find him. From what he knew of Clothilde Trahan, she *would* find him.

Nova Scotia was beginning to sound awfully tempting right now. He imagined for a moment arriving in Canada only to find the Trahan woman had beat him there.

Just listen.

"Please, stop for a moment, Monsieur Breaux."

Listen.

"All right," he said as much to her as to the gentle but insistent voice in his mind.

Theo stopped and turned to face her. She lagged only a few steps behind, a vision in blue, with the hated paper still crumpled in her hand.

"Say it," he demanded, pointing to the letter. "Go ahead. Laugh at me for not being able to read. I know you must find it highly amusing."

He affected a menacing stance, hands on hips and the worst grimace he could conjure up. After a moment, he noticed it had no effect on the girl. She stood very near, looking up with eyes shimmering with tears. To make matters worse, her bottom lip trembled.

Something inside crumbled.

His grimace melted, and he jammed his fists into his pants pockets. Looking away, he pretended to study the spiked leaves of a nearby palmetto.

It took every bit of gumption he had not to take her into his arms and soothe her strife. Instead, he reminded himself that this woman was dangerous. Not only did she know his secret, but she also held the key to a heart he'd locked up for its own protection.

Did he want to end up like his papa? Did he truly believe that seeing those brown eyes look up at him every morning and feeling those lips kiss him every night were worth putting away his traveling shoes and taking up the plow?

For a horrible moment, Theo actually considered the answer to both questions might be yes. Then good sense prevailed, and he shook off the crazy thought with a wave of his hand.

"I *said* I would stop, and I *did*. Speak your piece so I can get on home."

≈

What to say? Cleo bit her lip to keep it from trembling. She waited for something brilliant to come to mind, some word or phrase that would soothe the ruffled feelings of the carpenter. Instead, she could only think of how she might feel in the same circumstances.

"Well now, looks like I've done the impossible," Theophile said. "I've silenced the most talkative woman in Latagnier." He bowed from the waist in an imitation of courtly manners. "I'm so pleased to have been of service." With that, he turned and stalked away.

"Arête! Do you always run away like a coward?"

Did I just say that out loud?

The carpenter froze. Time seemed suspended. Even the birds ceased their chirping.

Cleo felt the letter crumple as her fingers squeezed her hand into a fist. She hurriedly stuffed the ruined paper into her apron pocket. Telling Uncle Joe she'd snooped and read the contents of his letter was the least of her worries at this point.

Theophile Breaux still stood with his back to her. Cleo carefully picked her way through the narrow path until she reached him. There was no going around him—the width of the path would not allow it—and turning back would brand her as much of a coward as he.

Her heart sank when she saw his shoulders slump.

The carpenter was *not* a coward. How awful of her to

think that, much less make the accusation aloud. Someone who tried so hard to cover up something embarrassing could only be thought of as courageous for making such an effort. That he would leave rather than continue a discussion on his inability to read seemed understandable.

What was wrong with her? She always said or did the wrong thing when she found herself in his presence.

Cleo reached out with a trembling hand to touch his sleeve. "I'm terribly, terribly sorry. I shouldn't have—"

"Shouldn't have what?" Jerking his arm away, he turned to face her. Despite the flash of fire in his eyes, his face appeared calm. "Shouldn't have told the truth? I suppose to you I *am* a coward, running away instead of staying here at this cabin and listening to you laugh at me."

She blinked back tears. "I never laughed at you."

The carpenter seemed to consider her statement for a moment before looking away. "I'll have the schoolhouse finished as quick as I can, and then I'll be gone." He swung his gaze back to meet hers. "Call it running or just getting away, but I intend to be on the first train out of town after this job is done."

Before she could respond, he turned and walked away. He'd gone a few yards down the path when he stopped abruptly and faced her once more.

"I'd be obliged if you'd not mention this to anyone. I'll be gone soon enough."

Gone. No more visits with the carpenter and no more casual suppers or coffees with her uncle. No more fussing and debating and apologizing for causing him to fall through the roof or step through a rotten porch board. No more teasing. No more pine needles in her hair or close encounters with overlarge cottonmouths.

No more Theophile Breaux.

She looked up into his face and felt her heart skid to a

stop. Before she could think better of it, she spoke the words that were on her heart.

"Monsieur Breaux, I don't want you to leave Latagnier."

Her statement seemed to take him by surprise as much as it did her. For a second he looked to be fumbling with his words. She, on the other hand, began wishing with all her might that she could reel hers back in.

"I don't see as how you have a say in the matter," he finally stated. *"Sa te regard pas."*

"Maybe I *am* making it concern me. What do you think about that?"

Cleo couldn't believe her own brazenness. Why, if this were any man other than Theophile Breaux, she might consider their exchange to be flirting.

"I try not to think about you at all, Mademoiselle Trahan."

He said it, but something in his demeanor gave Cleo serious doubts about whether he actually meant it.

Whirling around to make the short walk home, she wondered if she'd made a mistake. No matter what Theophile Breaux thought, he was stuck with her—at least until the schoolhouse was complete.

After that, only *le bon Dieu* knew for sure.

"I'll be back tomorrow to see how the renovations are progressing, Monsieur Breaux."

"Is that a promise or a threat, *cher*?" came his quick reply.

She stopped and suppressed a smile. "What did you call me?" she asked without turning around.

When he failed to respond, she headed for home. This time she wore a smile.

thirteen

Knee deep in the thicket with an aching foot, Theo tried to make sense of what he had just heard. The prettiest girl in Latagnier stood right there in front of him, calling him a coward one minute and asking him to stick around the next.

She seemed to think better of the words as soon as she spoke them, for she pressed past him and fled. But she left without taking the statement back, a sign she *did* mean what she said.

Then there was the business of calling her *cher*. That endearment hadn't come out of his mouth in regard to a woman in years.

He should have gone after her. He could have caught her in no time. She wasn't any bigger than a minute and wore those silly skirts that would more than slow her down.

But if he had, what would he have said? That he didn't want to leave her, either? That he'd stay?

While the first thought was true, the second was impossible. He and the Lord had a deal, and Clothilde Trahan was *not* a part of it.

He would miss her. That much was certain. But stay here in Latagnier, give up his plan to head for Nova Scotia? How could he do that for a mere slip of a girl?

He'd spend the rest of his life wondering if she was worth it. *No, you won't.*

Ignoring the insistent voice, Theo watched the Trahan woman's back until she disappeared up the path. When he could no longer see blue skirts and dark hair, Theo turned and headed back to the cabin. The schoolhouse, he corrected.

He'd have to start thinking of the place as a school. It was sure going to be one in short order.

That would make Mademoiselle Trahan very happy.

Once she saw his handiwork, she would forget all about thinking he ought to stick around. What did she have in mind for him anyway? Courting? That hardly seemed possible.

He'd fallen hard that night across the supper table, but since then he'd had no trouble keeping his distance. At least *he'd* managed to stay away.

She's the one who keeps ending up underfoot.

A thought dawned, and he stopped to savor it. Clothilde Trahan didn't want him to leave Latagnier, and she couldn't keep away from the schoolhouse.

What did those two things add up to?

Theo ducked under a low-hanging pine branch, then shook his head.

Nothing that made any sense. Logic told him the Trahan girl didn't have a brain in her head when it came to men, but his heart told him otherwise. Something in her words today showed her feelings—he just knew it.

Something that said she cared.

He headed back to the site with this thought still chasing him. Picking up the hammer to pound nails reminded him of the expression on her face when he'd been caught off guard while demolishing the wall. As he looked around, he realized just about everything at the schoolhouse reminded him of Clothilde Trahan.

He sighed. The whole idea of taking up with Joe Trahan's niece just seemed too far-fetched. What would a smart girl like her want with a dumb carpenter like him?

Ask her.

"Now that's the craziest thing I've heard in a long time," he said under his breath. "Crazier than thinking a girl like her would be interested in a man like me."

Still, he walked home with a spring in his step, or at least as much of a spring as he could manage with only one good foot. His sunny disposition carried him all the way to bedtime, when he finally laid his head down on his pillow and closed his eyes.

There, in the darkness, he generally met his Savior one last time before falling asleep. Tonight, however, thoughts of the day intruded.

Allowing the events of the afternoon to unfold once more in his mind, Theo recounted each word, every exchange of conversation between himself and Joe's niece.

As he fell into the blackness of sleep, he realized one important thing: Either he made it his business to court Clothilde Trahan, or he made it his business to leave her alone. Dangling between the two extremes like a puppet on a string would only lead to disaster.

❧

He awoke knowing he had to make a decision. Taking his time would be best, he decided, as something of this importance could not be rushed. He bade his mama and papa good-bye and headed off to the schoolhouse to see how much one man could get done in a day.

Along the way, his path somehow veered off, and he ended up on Joe Trahan's doorstep. Flo welcomed him in and poured his coffee, dealing him his fair share of eggs and bacon without asking if he wanted any. To his surprise, Clothilde joined them.

"*Bonjour*, Monsieur Breaux," she said as she breezed in, looking as if she'd taken all morning to get that pretty. Today she wore pink. It matched the color in her cheeks.

If he had his way, she'd never wear any other color.

Her braid lay coiled on the back of her head. Theo's fingers itched to set it free, to let the braid fall and release the blue-black strands altogether.

Would her hair fall in curls, or did she have straight, thick strands? He'd never seen it down around her shoulders, nor would a proper lady be seen that way. Still, whichever she possessed, he knew it would feel like silk in his hands.

"Monsieur Breaux," Flo said. *"Quoi y'a?"*

"Wrong? Nothing's wrong." When he realized the other three inhabitants of the kitchen were staring at him, he cast about for something to say. *"Bonjour,* Mademoiselle Clothilde," he finally said over the rim of his coffee cup as he watched her settle onto the seat across from him. *"Comment ça va?"*

"Very well, thank you, but please call me Cleo. Everyone else does."

"Cleo." Yes, he liked the sound of that. Clothilde was too sizable and formal for such a tiny thing. "All right, but only if you call me Theo."

"We rhyme." When his confusion showed, she shrugged. "Theo and Cleo. We rhyme."

"Yes," he said slowly. "I guess we do."

She nibbled at the corner of a piece of dry toast, then dabbed at her mouth with a napkin. "I'm surprised to see you here this morning." She paused to offer a radiant smile. "In light of our conversation yesterday, I mean."

Theo cleared his throat and gave Joe a sideways glance. He seemed to be taking in their exchange with interest. Thankfully, if he had any thoughts on the matter, he held his peace.

Their conversation of yesterday? What in the world was she up to?

Time to change the topic fast. Theo cast about for another item to discuss—something that didn't involve Clothilde Trahan, at least not directly.

"So, Joe, you got anything new to show me this morning?"

Joe seemed to think on the question a moment. "No," he said. "Nothing new this morning."

What? Joe Trahan with no new scribblings to show him? Nothing he'd figured since yesterday? Not likely. Theo met Cleo's direct gaze. Had she mentioned to her uncle that his carpenter couldn't read?

She gave him an innocent look, then reached for the sugar bowl. Dousing her coffee with several spoonfuls, she began to stir the black liquid in leisurely circles.

Her smile should have been a warning. Innocence like hers was dangerous. "Uncle Joe, Monsieur Breaux and I have a confession to make."

Theo nearly dropped his fork. "We do?"

Joe seemed to take particular interest in Cleo's statement. He pushed his spectacles onto his nose and peered at her, then turned his attention to Theo. "Oh?"

Cleo set a folded piece of paper on the table, then pushed it toward Joe. "This came yesterday."

"Is that right?" he asked. "Why am I just now getting it today? I thought I had all of the mail already. It looks like it's been read." He paused. "And fought over."

Cleo turned her substantial charm on her uncle. "Now that part's mostly my fault. You see, I was anxious and—"

"And so you snooped."

She nodded as Joe picked up the slightly crumpled sheet of paper and began to read. The mere act of watching someone else read generally gave Theo a range of mixed feelings. This morning, however, he only had one: dread.

"Well now," Joe said as his eyes scanned the page. "Isn't this interesting?" He peered over the paper to look at Theo. "What part did you play in this, son?"

Before Theo could answer, Cleo came to his rescue. "He didn't actually play an active part. His was more like a supporting role."

Joe shook his head. "Speak plain, child."

Cleo offered another radiant smile. "You see, when I read

that there would be a new teacher for the school, of course I wanted to go out and see if the place would be ready for her in time." She broadened her smile. "Well, it turns out there is a slight problem with that, isn't there, Theo?"

Joe turned to Theo as if he might be able to shed some light on the subject. Theo shrugged.

"The problem," Cleo continued, "is that the schoolhouse renovations will be completed well before the teacher's arrival."

"Is that right?" Joe asked him.

When Theo nodded, Joe turned his attention back to Cleo. "So what does that have to do with a problem at the schoolhouse? I'd say that the teacher arriving to a completed classroom is what we want."

Cleo shifted in her chair and stared at Theo. Again, innocence shone on her face. Again, he made a note to watch out for her. Pretty things came in small packages. . .but so did dynamite.

"Do you want to answer that?" When he shook his head, she continued. "The problem is that we will have a whole block of time that will be wasted if we wait until the teacher can come from New Orleans. The classroom will sit empty, and the children will be spending their time doing other things rather than learning."

"I see your point," Flo interjected.

Joe waved away her statement with a lift of his hand. "I don't." Once again, he turned to Theo. "Do you know what she's talking about?"

"Well," he said slowly, "actually I do." He took a bite of Flo's scrambled eggs and savored them while the three Trahans watched. When he could postpone his answer no longer, he nodded toward Cleo. "You have a schoolhouse almost finished and a whole passel of children who want to learn, right?"

"Right," Joe said.

"So what Cleo here is saying, is that she can take on the teacher's job until your friend from New Orleans shows up to relieve her from duty. The kids have a head start on their book learning, and Cleo stays out of trouble." He paused, ignoring the look on her face. "Well, at least she gets in less trouble, eh?"

Joe reached for his coffee mug and took a long drink of the stiff brew. Setting the cup back on the table, he turned his gaze on Flo. She smiled and nodded. A moment later, he echoed her gesture, then expanded it to a chuckle.

"I don't suppose it would hurt to have my niece teaching the children, at least until a proper teacher arrives," he said.

"Cleo, is that something you want to do?" Flo asked.

"*Oui,*" she said. "I want this very much, Tante Flo." She reached for her uncle's hand. "I promise I'll do a good job, Uncle Joe."

"Be careful what you promise," Joe said.

Funny, he was speaking to Cleo but looking at Theo.

Theo chewed another mouthful of eggs, then swiped at his mouth with the napkin. "I'd best be off," he declared as he rose. "I've got plenty to keep me busy today."

"I'm sure you do, dear," Flo said. "Do be careful out there. You never know what's going to happen."

"Especially with my niece on the loose." Joe pushed his spectacles back down on the bridge of his nose. He winked at Cleo, then picked up the newspaper. "Maybe I'll come out there later and check on your progress."

"That'd be fine, sir." Out of the corner of his eye, Theo saw Cleo watching them. "I'd welcome the chance to show you what I've been up to. I think you'll be surprised at how much progress has been made."

"Or maybe I'll just send Clothilde. Most days she seems to end up out there anyway." Joe seemed to take no notice of his niece's cry of protest as he lowered the paper a notch and peered over the pages.

"I wish you'd rethink that," Theo said, ignoring the urge to glance at Cleo to gauge her reaction. "It's awfully dangerous what with all the work going on out there, and Mademoiselle Trahan *is* a woman after all."

Joe paused a moment, then suppressed a smile as he stared down at Theo's sore foot. "I see your point."

"Well then, I'd best be off to work." He braved a look at Cleo, who stared back with no visible sign of emotion. Beside her, Flo sipped at her coffee, barely hiding a grin with her cup.

"Pleasure seeing you this morning, Theo," Flo said. "Give your mama and papa our best, will you? And tell them I'll be over tomorrow with a fresh mess of shelled peas."

He nodded. "Yes'm. I will."

Theo headed for the door like a hive of bees was on his tail. Nothing would please him more than to see Cleo Trahan's pretty face out at the schoolhouse every day. Unfortunately, nothing would be more dangerous—to his health and to his heart.

"Buck up, man," Theo said under his breath. "That girl's poison to your plans. One false step and you'll be heading to the church instead of Canada."

"Did you say something, Theo?"

"I'm sorry. What?" He whirled around to see Cleo standing in the doorway.

Arms wrapped around her middle, a smile decorated the Trahan girl's face. She took a couple of tentative steps toward him, then leaned against the porch rail and wrapped her fingers around the post.

"Who—me, say something? No." *Not to you, anyway.*

"That's funny," she said. "I thought I heard you say something about Canada."

His breath froze in his throat. What else had she heard?

"Canada? *Oui*. It's nice there this time of year," he said, hoping the casualness in his response hid the truth of his feelings. "A little chilly but nice."

She looked perplexed. *Good. Maybe she will think I'm one of those old men who talks to himself, and she'll steer clear of me.*

"Yes, well, thank you for speaking to Uncle Joe on my behalf," she said. "I hope that now I will get a chance to show him what I can do."

"I'll do my part and get the place in shape as quick as I can."

He turned and set off down the road, wondering if she still stood on the porch watching. As he turned toward the path leading to the schoolhouse, he glanced back to see she did.

"Theo, boy, you are in a whole heap of trouble," he said as the Trahan place disappeared behind the thicket.

fourteen

"*Allons*, you lazy thing. Get up from your nap in that hammock, and let's go fishing. You're wasting a perfectly good Sunday afternoon."

Theo lifted one eyelid to see his brother Alphonse staring down at him. If the truth were known, he'd been wide awake well before the skinny kid had begun stomping around the far end of the porch in the process of gathering his fishing gear.

"*Arête.*"

"No, I don't believe I'll stop." Alphonse balanced the net in his hand, then swung it like a tennis racket within inches of Theo's head. "*Vien ici*, big brother. The big ones'll be biting this afternoon. I feel it in my bones."

"Those bones of yours are going to find themselves broken if you come near me with that net again." Leaning up on one elbow, Theo balanced himself on the wobbling hammock, then fired a nasty look at his brother. "Unlike *you*, who snored like Great-granny Delchamp's old bulldog, *I* stayed awake during the pastor's sermon this morning."

Alphonse shrugged and tossed the net over his shoulder. "You're absolutely right, Theo." He paused to gather up the net and his cane pole. "But then I'd stay awake, too, if the girl I was sweet on sat three rows ahead of me on the right in a pretty yellow dress with a bow in her hair."

Theo fairly flew out of the hammock, causing Alphonse to make tracks to the other side of the porch, then off into the yard. "Has it ever occurred to you that I might be staying awake to hear what Pastor Broussard has to say?"

His brother seemed to consider Theo's statement for a moment. When a smile broke out on the boy's face, Theo braced himself for the smart-aleck answer he knew he was about to hear.

"Has it ever occurred to you that I might be taking a nap in church to let Pastor Broussard's message sink in deeper? I read something about that somewhere. Scientists think we learn just as much when we're asleep as when we're awake, sometimes more. Why just last Friday night I dreamed about Joseph and the coat of many colors. Wasn't that in last week's sermon?"

Theo nodded and relaxed his stance. "I believe it was."

Alphonse took a step backward. "So what part of the sermon were you dreaming about last night when you kept calling the name of Cleo Trahan?"

Theo lit out across the porch and down the steps, taking care to favor his injured foot. He made a dive for his brother just in time to let him get away. Alphonse ran cackling with laughter until he disappeared behind the house.

A few minutes later, Theo heard Alphonse calling to the little guys, then watched the trio head toward the bayou for an afternoon of fishing. As one last hurrah, Alphonse turned and saluted him with the cane pole.

"All hail, King Theophile," he called. "See him pine away on the porch, wishing he could make Cleo Trahan his queen."

Stomping across the grass, Theo pretended to give chase. Alphonse broke out in a run, the younger brothers following in hot pursuit.

Theo laughed at his brother's antics. He'd have to slug him if he caught him, so allowing the kid to think he could outrun his big brother served two purposes. It got rid of Alphonse without hurting him, and it left Theo with peace and quiet.

Just in case Alphonse had a mind to return, Theo hobbled

around the perimeter of the porch a few times before settling back into the hammock. He was about to close his eyes when he spied a flash of color coming up the road from the far end of the property.

Sitting up, he narrowed his eyes and tried to make out the identity of the one who walked toward the house. As the person drew nearer, he pegged her for a female—most likely one of his numerous aunts or cousins—clad in a light-colored dress.

"Figures," he said under his breath.

After all, the house was quiet, the boys were fishing, and Mama and the girls were away making visits. Why wouldn't he and Papa have their naps interrupted by kinfolk?

Theo groaned. *Another reason to head on down the road as soon as possible.*

A man needed his Sunday afternoon nap, or Monday morning just didn't start right. Once Monday was ruined, the rest of the week generally followed suit.

"Before you know it, a whole week's lost and all for want of a nap."

He decided to pretend deep sleep in the hopes that whichever aunt or cousin arrived on the doorstep would not disturb him. After all, no woman—Cajun or otherwise—who'd been raised right would wake up a workingman on a Sunday afternoon, leastways not in his opinion.

So he settled back and headed for dreamland, only occasionally taking a peek from beneath his eyelids to check the visitor's progress. She wore yellow and carried a package under her arm.

How nice. At least she thought to bring something.

"I hope it's a pie," he murmured as he snuggled deeper into the softness of the hammock. "One good thing about being back in Latagnier. A man can sure eat good here."

He cast one last glance at whichever aunt or cousin

approached, then closed his eyes. What seemed only a moment later, he awoke with a start. The woman was within spitting distance of the house before his tired brain made the connection.

Yellow.

Cleo Trahan.

He sat up so fast, it made his head spin. Actually it spun the hammock, too, landing him rear-end first on the porch floor. Theo scrambled up and landed on his sore foot.

For a minute, he gave serious consideration to heading indoors to hide or taking to the woods in the hopes she might give up and go home. But before she went home, most likely she'd run into at least one family member.

Wouldn't Papa have fun talking to her? First thing you know, his father would be spilling all sorts of information, not the least of which would be his opinion about the fact that his eldest son was well past twenty-five and still unmarried. Then he'd surely inquire as to whether Mademoiselle Trahan had a steady beau. After that, who knew what can of worms Papa would open?

Well, Theo just wouldn't let that happen.

Groaning, he hobbled off the porch. The foot that seemed to be healing now felt worse than yesterday.

Further proof that Cleo Trahan was a menace.

Better to head her off than to take the chance that she might be spotted by one of the family. The brothers were fishing, Papa was napping, and the ladies were visiting, but around here, you never knew when a relative would pop out of the woodwork.

The last thing he needed was to have one of the family see him visiting with Cleo Trahan. He might be closer to thirty than twenty, but teasing from his family still plagued him. He had a mind not to hear more of it on the Lord's Day.

Cleo waved and picked up her pace. *"Bonjour."*

To compensate, Theo had to hurry along, as well—not an easy thing, considering the shooting pain in his foot. His gaze shifted from his guest to the package she carried in the crook of her arm.

"Well now. This is a surprise."

She shifted the package to her other arm and looked up at him, eyes wide. "I'd hoped to speak to you after church this morning, but you were gone before I could reach you."

"Yes, well, I tend to slip out quickly."

"I've noticed."

Her smile should have pleased him. Instead it set his warning bells off. An awkward silence fell between them. He could stand here all day and look at her. He also needed to send her home.

Only the sound of children's laughter set him in motion. "Why don't you and I find someplace quiet and set a spell?"

"That would be lovely."

Lovely? She had no idea.

Taking her by the elbow, Theo led his visitor toward the nearest source of cover—a stand of oak trees just ahead on their left.

"The bayou is so pretty this time of year," she said as she allowed him to guide her to a secluded spot beside a crook in the bayou.

So are you, he could have added.

Theo looked both directions before choosing a little grassy place beside the water. "Here, how about you and me sit over there?" He pointed to an upended cedar log, a natural bench he and Alphonse had found just that past week.

With no sign of the fishermen and no more noise from the women, he felt almost certain they could have a measure of privacy. Now if he could just get the woman to speak her piece and go on home.

Once she settled herself on the log, the Trahan woman

placed the package in her lap, then waited for him to take a seat beside her. She traced the length of the string-tied package and picked at the brown paper wrapping.

"I have a gift for you." She bit her lip and looked away. "I hope you like it."

A fish jumped with a plop, sending ripples out from the center of the black bayou water. Theo watched the circle widen and tried to think of the right way to send this sweet girl back home without accepting her gift. If he took whatever she brought him, he'd be beholden to her, and that just wouldn't do.

He finally braved a look down into a face that beamed with happiness. Once again, his heart sunk.

How easy it would be to let himself fall in love with her. Not just be smitten, as he'd been ever since their dinner together several weeks ago, but actually be in once-in-a-lifetime love. No, he'd begun to believe that he might actually be able to spend the rest of his life with this woman.

Happily, no less.

Theo shrugged off the frightening thought with a roll of his shoulders. "How come you bring me a present, Cleo, eh?"

Cleo continued to toy with the wrappings. Finally she smiled. "I have several reasons, actually." She paused and seemed to be considering her words. "First, I feel I owe you a debt of gratitude for all you've done."

"Aw, I haven't done anything."

She shook her head. "That's not true. Way back at the beginning, you could have told my uncle on me, and you didn't. You brought back the basket I left at the schoolhouse, even though it meant you got soaked by the storm."

He lifted a finger as if to make an important point. "I'll admit you're right about the first one, but I got a shrimp dinner out of bringing that basket to you. I'll tell you something. Your aunt's shrimp étouffée makes me want to fetch more baskets.

I'd never admit it to my mama, but I hadn't thought anybody could best her in a cooking contest until now."

"Actually," she said slowly as she gave him a sideways glance, "I cooked the shrimp."

"Did you now?"

Well, this was some news. Pretty as a newborn foal, and she could cook, too? Good thing he was sitting down. His knees were feeling a little wobbly.

fifteen

"I love to cook. I do it every day."

What a dumb thing to say, Cleo thought. She sounded like a foolish girl trying her hand at flirting for the first time.

Immediately ashamed, she looked away. While she could admit to cooking daily, saying she loved it was a bit of an exaggeration. She'd grown up at her aunt's side, helping to cut buttermilk biscuit dough with an iced-tea glass and learning to stir up a roux for thickening before she could spell her own name.

Cooking was, well, merely what ladies did. There was nothing remarkable about this, at least nothing worth mentioning. And yet she *had* mentioned it. Perhaps she *was* a foolish girl trying her hand at flirting.

The carpenter nodded, seemingly interested. His grin made her toes tingle. "I like to eat every day, so I guess we've got that in common."

"Right." She stretched her legs out in front of her and flexed her feet.

A soft breeze blew past, on it the scent of spring and the promise of summer. Two tiny ladybugs landed on the toe of her shoe and began to crawl in circles. She wiggled her foot, and they flew off together.

Cleo clamped her lips tight and fought the urge to offer any further attempts at conversation. Who knew what less-than-witty statement she might make next time?

The man beside her said nothing but rather seemed to be studying a single fluffy cloud as it floated past above the tree line. They sat in silence for what seemed like an eternity.

"Can you bake a pie?"

Startled, she nodded. "Sure. Why?"

He shrugged and reached over to pick a strand of wild honeysuckle off the vine. "Just wondering."

"Oh. Any particular kind you like best?"

"Nope."

So much for that discussion. Cleo drummed her fingers on the parcel in her lap and watched the bayou ripple past. Two marsh birds landed on the low-slung branch of a dogwood on the opposite bank, while a couple of fish jumped like synchronized swimmers.

Cleo sighed. Was it her imagination, or was it true that everywhere she looked today, things seemed paired off?

Sometimes it gave her pause to think what it might be like to be a part of a pair, maybe with someone big and handsome like the man seated next to her. Most days, however, she remembered that hers was a higher calling.

To be a teacher meant she would have to give up any thoughts of pairing up with any man. A married teacher didn't last long, for soon babies came along and the career was over.

Uncle Joe had already proven that getting qualified teachers in Latagnier was a difficult proposition at best. Just because this woman from New Orleans agreed to come didn't mean she would. And if she did take the job, how long would she stay?

"Daydreaming?"

Cleo startled, and the package landed at her feet. "I'm sorry. I do that sometimes. I was thinking about being a teacher."

He nodded. "From what I can tell, you think about that a lot."

"*Oui.*" She collected the gift and placed it in his hands. "Here. I brought you this."

At first he seemed reluctant, holding the item at arm's length as if he were trying to recognize it. "What's this for? It's not my birthday, and Christmas is a long way off."

"Open it and see." Her heart picked up its pace. What if coming here was a mistake? "Go ahead," she added. "It won't bite. I promise."

Weighing it in his hands, he turned to face her. "Well now, considering I've already braved a cottonmouth for you, I shouldn't be surprised if it did bite."

He stood and reached into his pocket for a small knife, then settled back onto the log beside her to make short work of the string. The paper fell off, revealing his gift.

Her father's well-worn copy of *Pilgrim's Progress*.

"A book?" His tone was flat, his expression one of disbelief. "You gave me a *book*. Me?"

"Not just any book. This one belonged to my father." Cleo took a deep breath and let it out slowly. "*Pilgrim's Progress* was one of his favorites, although I never did count it as one of mine. In any case, I wanted you to have it."

"Why?" Theo met her gaze, then leaned toward her. A flash of anger clouded his features. "Is this a joke?"

"A joke? No." She paused to compose her thoughts, then plunged headlong into the reason she'd invited herself to visit this afternoon. "You see, I thought that perhaps I could. . .well, that is, if you were willing, you could let me. . ."

Understanding seemed to dawn. His features twisted into a smile, but there was no joy in his eyes. "You thought I might let you teach me to read. Is that it?"

She nodded. Suddenly her brilliant idea didn't sound so brilliant after all. "You're an intelligent man, Theo. I think you'd learn quickly, even if you are a little more advanced in years than the others I'll be teaching."

"Do you now?" He rose and turned to help her up. "Do you really think an old man like me capable of learning, Mademoiselle Teacher? After all, I'm considerably older than your average student."

"You're not old. What are you, twenty-two, twenty-three?"

Theo straightened his shoulders and looked away. "I'll be twenty-seven come June."

Her expression of surprise gave him a certain satisfaction. Maybe now she would see that. . .that what? That he was old and ignorant? That she'd do better spending her time with people her own age instead of someone nearly nine years older?

As much as this information might achieve his goal of running her off, it gave a certain sting to his pride. Theo decided to put an end to the foolishness and just state things as plainly as possible.

"I can't accept this gift." He paused as he tried to think of the nicest way possible to get rid of the book—and of her. "So now that you know this, you can go on home."

She looked more stunned than hurt. "Is there a reason?"

Other than his trampled dignity? *"Merci beaucoup,* Cleo," he said as he thrust the book in her direction. "But you need to go home now."

She ignored the offer of the book and touched his sleeve. "Have I offended you?"

How he longed to light into her, to scream and yell and make all sorts of noise letting her know just how she'd injured his pride. If only he hadn't been raised a gentleman.

"Pas du tout," he said instead. "If I were offended, I would state so."

Afraid. Now that came closer to how he felt. Afraid of making a fool of himself, afraid of spending time with her, and afraid he might be giving up everything he wanted for something he never knew he needed.

"So this was all just a misunderstanding." She settled back on the log and gave him an expectant look, patting the empty place beside her. "Tante Flo's not expecting me until suppertime. If you'd like, we could begin by learning the vowel sounds."

Her glee grated on his resolve. So did her enthusiasm. The

urge to sit beside her on the log all afternoon, whether for learning vowels or just watching the clouds float by, hit him hard. He squeezed the book so hard he was afraid he might soon hear the pilgrim squeal in protest.

"Come sit down, Theo, and we'll get started."

He almost gave in, almost had himself convinced. Almost—but not quite.

Taking a step back, Theo felt his mind reel with the possibility of what could happen to his dreams. His gaze scanned the perimeter, searching out any means of escape.

He found none. Either he told her the truth and risked upsetting her, or he sat down beside her and risked his freedom.

Whichever way he looked at it, spending another minute with Cleo Trahan was a bad idea. Time to get rid of her.

Dumping the book into her lap, he took yet another step back. "Please just go." He spoke the words through clenched jaw, unsure whether he'd said them plainly enough to be understood. When the first tear glistened in the corner of her eye, he knew he'd been heard.

"Stop that," he demanded. "Take your book and your tears and go home."

Without looking back, he stalked away. Anger set him on the path for home, but his conscience put up a roadblock that his mind—and his feet—couldn't get past.

Theo stopped in his tracks and turned around. As much as he didn't want to admit it, he owed Cleo Trahan an apology. He also owed her an explanation, but only if she asked.

Better she accept his apology and head for Joe's place with the book in tow. Better yet if she were already on her way home.

Even though Cleo might think otherwise, she really did not want him to tell her the why of things. Worse, he really did not want to admit it.

Theo stalked down the path and pushed past the low-lying limbs and thicket, all the while daring to hope that he wouldn't find the Trahan girl still waiting for him. His hopes were dashed when he spied her standing where he'd left her.

Before he could say a word, she lifted her hand as if to silence him. "I just have one question. Answer it, and I'll go."

He walked closer, dangerously closer, until she stood so near that he could reach out and. . .no, he didn't dare think what he could do with her within arm's reach. "Just one question?"

Leaning back slightly to look up at him, she nodded.

"All right," he said slowly. "But even though I can't read, I *can* count. You only get one chance, and I'm only going to answer one question. Now speak your piece so we can both get on home."

She blinked hard, then straightened her shoulders and drew herself up to her full height—still pitifully less than his. "One question. Why? If it bothers you that you can't read, and it obviously does, then why not let me teach you? It's what I do."

Emotions swirled and seethed just beneath the surface. Wanting to say yes, needing to say no, wanting her to stay, needing her to leave. Theo's skin tingled, and he felt hot and cold at the same time. He hadn't been this miserable since he weathered the chicken pox nearly twenty years ago.

"You want to know why I won't let you teach me to read?"

She nodded, and the sun caught her hair, glinting off the blue-black strands. "Yes, that's all I want to know," she said as she thrust the brown leather volume in his direction. "Take this book and look at it, then tell me you don't want me to teach you to read what's inside of it."

Theo removed the book from her hand and set it on the log without opening it. "I'm too old for this, Cleo. I'm heading for Canada first chance I get, and nothing's going to interfere with that."

Dark brows drew together as his companion gave him a perplexed look. "I don't understand what learning to read has to do with—"

"You're right. You *don't* understand. You're young and naive, and you don't have any idea what you're doing to me. I can't spend five minutes with you and keep my conscience clear and my plans straight. Unless you can show me everything I need to know in under five minutes, teaching me to read is out of the question."

Taking two steps back, Theo stuffed his hands into his pants pockets, as much for his own protection as for hers. He would never hurt her, but at this moment, he couldn't be held to any sort of proper conduct. His fingers itched to wrap her in his arms and hold her, and the way those lips pouted, why, he could hardly stand not kissing them.

Of course, he could do neither.

"There, I answered your question," he said a might gentler. "Now go. Please."

"Please listen."

"Go home." He barely spoke the words through his clenched jaw. Did he say them to Cleo or to himself?

If she stayed, he might have to admit he loved her. If she left, well, that would be the best thing for both of them. Then she would merely be a fond memory instead of a serious problem.

Theo caught his breath and held it. If only he could catch his feelings so easily. Cleo stepped toward him, arms outstretched, and the tightly strung wire that held his emotions in check snapped.

"Theo, I—"

Before she could complete the sentence, he took her in his arms. Just to hold her. No harm in that. Just for a second.

And then he kissed her.

sixteen

Cleo reeled back, her hand covering her mouth. Her first kiss, and it was awful.

Well, not exactly awful, but it was uninvited and unexpected, and it served to awaken something inside her. Never again could she wonder what her first kiss would be like.

Theo held her against him, her ear pressed against his chest such that she could hear his heart thumping wildly. Hers took up the pace until she felt it might burst.

So this was how love felt. She looked up into the eyes of the carpenter, expecting to find some sign that the kiss had changed him. That he felt the same.

Instead she saw a blank stare followed in quick succession by what looked like anger and then regret—none of the tender emotions she expected. Whatever the reason he might claim for kissing her, it certainly did not seem like love.

"I shouldn't have done that," he whispered, his voice husky and deep. "Please. . .just. . .go. . .now."

She willed the tears not to fall as she pulled away from his grasp. *Just wait, Cleo. You can't cry in front of him.*

Straightening her spine, she turned and walked away with what little pride she had left. As soon as she knew he could no longer see her, she picked up her skirts and broke into a run.

With tears staining her face, she knew she couldn't go home. Instead, she headed for the only other place of solace she could think of on a Sunday afternoon besides the church—the schoolhouse. No one would look for her there.

Racing up the steps, she threw open the door, then stepped inside and slammed it shut. The place smelled like new wood and old paint, a strange but comfortable combination. Cleo leaned against the wall. Finally the emotions proved too much. She sank to the floor and cried like a baby.

Somewhere along the way, the door must have opened, for Cleo opened her eyes to see Theo standing there. Silhouetted by the brilliant sunshine behind him, he looked like a dark and ominous shadow. *How fitting*, she thought.

"I'm so sorry."

Gone was the voice made deep and husky by emotion. In its place was the flat and cold sound of a man without feeling. Cleo could find no answer for his statement, so she remained silent.

He moved closer but only slightly so, edging to within reach of her. Setting the book beside her, he straightened and looked away.

"*Arête*. Please don't cry."

She didn't want to stop, didn't want to give in to what she knew came next—the forgiveness. Again, she said nothing, although she did swipe at her tear-stained cheeks with the hem of her apron.

He began to pace, then stopped short. "Cleo, I don't know what happened." Shaking his head, he pounded his fist against the door. "That's not true. I *do* know what happened."

Cleo watched him as he stood looking out the window. He grimaced, then turned his attention to her.

"I'm a fool, Cleo, and I know that," he said as he crossed the distance to her and offered his hand to pull her into a standing position.

She accepted his help with caution, pulling away as soon as he released his grip. Standing so close brought the fresh memories back, first of the kiss and then of the regret she saw on his face immediately afterward.

He still wore that regret.

Cleo wrapped her hands around her waist and fixed her

gaze on his eyes, fighting the urge to look away. "I'm going to give you the same advice you gave me, Theo," she somehow managed to say. "Advice I should have taken."

Regret shifted to confusion, and he shook his head. "What's that?"

"Go home."

She turned to walk away only to see that she had nowhere to go. A large desk that had been partially dismantled blocked the back door. Several long benches were stacked atop its expansive surface. The furnishings of her schoolroom, she realized.

Escaping with what little remained of her dignity seemed the only route to take. Cleo squared her shoulders and walked back into the main room, where Theo waited. He'd begun to pace again but halted when he caught sight of her.

"I'm leaving," she said. "Do follow my advice and go home." She reached down to snatch up the book and cradle it in her arm.

Theo stepped between her and freedom. "Just hear me out," he said. "I'm real bad at this, but I'd like to try and make sense of things before you run off mad."

"Mad?" She fought for control of her voice. "You think I'm mad?"

He shrugged. "Well, if I were in your place, I'd be mad as a hornet. I mean, a man takes liberties—"

"Who is taking liberties?"

Cleo looked past to see Uncle Joe and the pastor standing in the door. She pasted on a smile and sashayed past Theo to head toward the pair. When she reached her uncle, she gave him a quick peck on the cheek, being careful to keep her red-rimmed eyes closed until she'd safely passed him.

"No one's taking liberties, Uncle Joe," she said over her shoulder. "Theo and I were just discussing a book."

She stopped to turn and face the three men. Of the

trio, the carpenter was the only one whose face wore no expression. The other two smiled as if they shared a secret.

"If you'll excuse me, I'll be taking this book back home." She gave Theo a direct look. "Wouldn't want something so special to end up in the hands of someone who didn't appreciate it."

As her feet hit the dirt and pointed toward home, she wondered why she'd bothered to save Theophile Breaux's hide. One word to Uncle Joe and the pastor about the kiss and the carpenter would have been in trouble up to his eyeballs.

She didn't have to wonder long. The truth caught up with her before she reached the front porch of Uncle Joe's place. She didn't tell on Theo because she wanted him to kiss her again.

And again.

"Oh my," she said as she climbed the porch steps. "Well, that will never do."

"What will never do?"

Cleo looked up to see Tante Flo sitting in the parlor, her Bible open on the rosewood table before her. She leaned down to embrace her aunt, then slipped the tattered copy of *Pilgrim's Progress* back into its place on the bookshelf beside the fireplace.

Tante Flo closed the Bible and gave Cleo a sideways look. "I asked you what would never do."

She smiled. "Anything that interferes with me becoming a teacher will never do."

"I'm glad to hear it," Tante Flo said. "I've wondered a time or two what would have happened if I had put my teaching ahead of love."

Surprised, Cleo feigned a casual attitude. "And what did you decide?"

Tante Flo smiled. "I decided that when the Lord puts the right man in your path, it doesn't matter what you're giving up. It's always a better-than-even exchange."

Cleo settled onto the settee and slipped off her shoes, tucking her feet beneath her. "How did you know that Uncle Joe was the right man?"

Her aunt leaned closer and shook her head. "I didn't," she said. "In fact, I thought he was the most exasperating man I had ever met."

Now this was interesting. After two decades of marriage, Flo and her husband seemed to be more in love than ever. Cleo assumed they'd always felt this way.

"I don't believe it," she finally said. "I've never heard you say a cross word to Uncle Joe. How could you find him exasperating?"

"Well, to start, he ran off every other beau I had."

Cleo giggled. "He did? How?"

"By planting himself in my kitchen every morning and sharing coffee with my papa. Before long, Papa didn't want any other man around except your uncle Joe. Said they were all beneath me or some such nonsense, but I always knew Joe was giving my daddy an earful and turning him against anybody but himself."

"That's pretty underhanded, Tante Flo. I'm surprised at Uncle Joe."

"Oh, Cleo, nothing should surprise you when it comes to love." She paused to run her finger over the cracked spine of the Bible. "See, he made friends with the papa, but he was really there to see the daughter." She paused and winked. "Much like our Monsieur Breaux, I believe."

"What are you talking about? You and I both know he comes here to talk to Uncle Joe about the schoolhouse project. How else would he get the updates and the changes in plans? It's much more convenient for him to come by on his way to the schoolhouse than for Uncle Joe to go all the way out there later in the day."

As she protested, her mind reeled back to the kiss and its aftermath, the sound of his heart racing against her ear, and the feel of his arms around her. The color flooded her cheeks, and the room suddenly felt a bit too warm.

Tante Flo rose and brushed past Cleo to stand at the window. A moment later she settled beside her on the settee and took Cleo's hand in hers.

"He's kissed you, hasn't he?"

seventeen

Cleo stuttered and sputtered and finally made an excuse not to answer her aunt. She'd never lie—she couldn't—for her aunt knew her too well. Racing to her room, she poured fresh water in the basin and washed her face. As she toweled her heated cheeks dry, she studied her face for signs she'd changed.

Nothing out of the ordinary greeted her. Same plain face, same drab brown eyes, same hair—dark as bayou water and just as unruly.

Falling onto her bed, she stared up at the ceiling. Whatever got into her this afternoon, it would just have to get out. She had no time for love and certainly not for loving such an ornery creature as Theophile Breaux.

It was bad enough he'd kissed her, but to regret it afterward? Well, that just wouldn't do. She had half a mind to search him out and tell him so.

She rose. Yes, that's just what she'd do. She would find the fellow and give him what for. How dare he play with her affections? Surely he knew what sort of emotions he would stir up when he held her. Surely he, who was much older than she as it turned out, would know very well the results of emotions left to run free.

"Oh, Cleo, if you aren't the most dramatic thing in Latagnier, I don't know who is," she whispered as she fell against the mattress once more.

"You all right in there?" she heard Tante Flo call.

"Yes, ma'am," she responded quickly. "Just having a Sunday afternoon nap."

"Well, get up right now and come help me see to supper.

Sunday afternoon's gone and evening's coming." Her footsteps stopped at the closed door. "Your uncle's going to come home hungry and wonder what happened to his dinner. And unless I miss my guess, he'll have the pastor with him, too."

"Yes, ma'am," she repeated as she rose and walked to the basin to give her face another quick scrubbing. Tante Flo might have suspected a kiss, but she'd stand and scrub all day if she had to in order to keep Uncle Joe from knowing.

She needn't have worried. Uncle Joe seemed too preoccupied with discussing the finer points of planed wood with the pastor to notice any change in his niece. Listening to snatches of conversation, her ears took special notice whenever the name of the carpenter was mentioned.

A few times, the men included her in the conversation, asking her opinion about books and other items of interest to the new teacher. Uncle Joe even mentioned the teachers' college, hinting that he thought an education of that sort to be good for a woman in some cases.

Cleo went to bed, praying the Lord would cause Uncle Joe to believe she was one of those cases. Of course, as she closed her eyes and embraced the fog of sleep, it wasn't Uncle Joe and a possible education at the teachers' college that filled her mind.

It was Theophile Breaux.

Irritating, presumptuous, handsome, stubborn Theophile Breaux.

"Go away," she whispered to his memory.

The Theo in her dreams didn't listen any more than the real Theo had. As she gave way to the blackness of sleep, she remembered the kiss.

And in her dreams, he kissed her again.

And this time it wasn't awful at all.

When she awoke, she tried to remember every detail of the

dream. Then, as she headed to the kitchen to help her aunt make breakfast, she tried to forget it.

Uncle Joe spied Theo coming across the clearing before she did. "Set another place, Flo," he said with a chuckle. "Here comes our regular morning visitor."

Tante Flo sent a smile toward Cleo, then reached into the cupboard for another plate and coffee mug. A moment later, silverware clanked against the tabletop.

"Reminds me of someone I once knew," Tante Flo said.

"Does it now?" Uncle Joe chuckled. "Was he a handsome fellow, this man?"

"Why yes, he was." Her aunt paused from setting the table to give her uncle a kiss on his balding head. "In fact, he still is."

To be in love like these two. Would she ever know that kind of happiness? To banish the thought, Cleo busied herself with the pancake batter until she found her hands were fumbling terribly and allowing shells to fall into the mixture.

"Go fetch us some more eggs, child," her aunt said. "I'm afraid what we got here won't be enough at this rate."

She cast a glance out the window, then back at Tante Flo. To fetch eggs meant to walk right past Theo Breaux. Surely her aunt knew that.

So Tante Flo was matchmaking?

"It won't work," she whispered as she leaned toward her aunt.

Just before the screen door closed, Cleo heard her aunt say, "It might."

She picked up her pace and kept her gaze focused on the ground. If she didn't look him in the eyes, perhaps he'd walk past and go on inside. Surely he'd come to see Uncle Joe and not her, anyway.

Stepping a little faster, she braved a glance up at his face. Unlike yesterday, he wore a look of relief.

At what? Probably at the fact that I'm not sitting inside waiting on him.

"*Bonjour,*" she said as she passed him.

"Might what?" Theo motioned toward the screen door. "What was your aunt talking about?"

Cleo shook her head and returned her concentration to the ground beneath her swiftly moving feet. "Nothing," she called.

"Cleo, wait. *Arête.*"

"No time, Theo." She reached for the latch on the chicken coop with trembling hands. Why did she let that man affect her?

When she returned from the henhouse, she deposited the egg basket on the sideboard, then fled the kitchen to begin her chores. Sweeping came first, so she found the broom and began in the parlor, the farthest point from the kitchen she could find.

"Cleo," Uncle Joe called. "Could you fetch my spectacles, *cher?*"

"*Oui.*"

She set the broom aside to retrieve her uncle's glasses from the table beside the settee. Stepping inside the kitchen, she saw both men pause from their conversation to look up at her. While her uncle regarded her with a warm smile, his guest showed no emotion.

"*Merci beaucoup, cher,*" Uncle Joe said. "Now would you warm up this coffee a bit? I've done so much jawing with this young man here that I've let mine get cold." He turned to face Theo. "You need Cleo to warm you up, too?"

The carpenter looked like he'd swallowed a bug. "No," he sputtered.

Cleo brought the coffeepot to the table and filled Uncle Joe's cup, watching the steam rise off the liquid and feeling the heat rise from her cheeks. Surely Uncle Joe hadn't intended to say *that*. She glanced at his face to see that her uncle was trying not to laugh.

Well, of all the nerve.

She straightened her spine and set the pot between them on the dish towel. "If you don't need anything else, I'll get back to my chores."

Uncle Joe prodded Theo. "You need her for anything?"

Their gazes collided. For a long moment, Cleo could do nothing but stare into the carpenter's dark eyes. Then he looked away and offered her uncle a smile.

"Can't think of anything. Now, what were you saying about that beam over the old parlor?"

"Well then, I'll just go back to what I was doing." She spoke to Uncle Joe, but her gaze was firmly fixed on Theophile Breaux. How dare he dismiss her as if he hadn't kissed her just yesterday?

"That's real fine, Cleo," Uncle Joe said.

The carpenter, however, said nothing.

Cleo turned on her heels and stomped away. "Humph," she muttered as she turned and headed down the hall.

"What was that?" Uncle Joe called.

"Nothing."

Cleo went back to her sweeping with renewed vigor. Part of her felt relieved that the carpenter pretended nothing had transpired between them. Another part of her felt righteous indignation at his blatant disregard for the feelings he'd caused to surface.

"What are you complaining about?" She reached to pull the settee away from the wall. "You got what you wanted. A teacher can't fall in love, so this is all for the better."

This thought sustained her until Uncle Joe once more called her to come into the kitchen. This time when she stepped inside the room, she noticed her uncle was alone. Theo must have left quietly, or perhaps her rather intense sweeping and moving of furniture had been noisier than she thought.

"Did you call me, Uncle Joe?"

"I did." He indicated the chair beside him, the spot Theo had recently vacated. "Sit down a minute, will you?"

Cleo complied, trying not to notice the chair still felt warm. Obviously the carpenter hadn't made his departure very long ago. She looked past her uncle to the window to see if she could spot him.

"He went the other way."

Turning her gaze on her uncle, she shook her head. "What are you talking about?"

"Theo. He went the other way."

She shrugged. "Didn't ask."

Uncle Joe smiled. "Didn't have to." He pushed his spectacles up on his forehead and regarded her with a serious look. "Cleo, I want you to know that your aunt and I have felt the Lord blessed us with a daughter of our own when you came to live with us. From the day you came through the door, you've had my heart. Did you know that?"

Had she? Cleo blinked back a tear. "Thank you for telling me this."

Uncle Joe covered her hand with his, then entwined his fingers with hers. "Flo and I love you, and we want what's best. Do you believe that?"

"Yes, sir."

"Then I hope you'll understand and forgive those times when I want to coddle you and treat you like a child. In my mind, I know you're a grown woman, but in my heart, you're still that curly-headed three-year-old who used to fall asleep on my shoulder in that big old rocking chair in the parlor."

The image of her uncle gathering her into his arms to rock her to sleep rose in her mind. She smiled.

"That's why it's so hard to say this."

Cleo's attention snapped back to Uncle Joe. "Say what?"

He looked away and fidgeted with the edge of the table. "Well, like I said, you're a grown woman." His gaze swung back to meet hers. "You still intend to make a teacher of yourself?"

Concern etched her thoughts. Had he changed his mind about allowing her to take on the teaching position at the Latagnier school?

"Yes." She bit her lip to keep from saying more.

"Then I think you ought to be trained proper." He shifted positions and tightened his grip on her hand. "Once your replacement arrives at the end of the summer, I'd like to send you off to get that fancy education you've talked about."

"At the teachers' college?"

She flung herself at her uncle and wrapped her arms around his neck. "Oh, thank you, Uncle Joe. Thank you, thank you."

"Well, looks like you gave her the news."

Cleo looked up to see the carpenter standing in the door. He pulled on the screen door and stepped inside, crossing the kitchen in a few long strides to deposit a broken piece of wood on the table.

Cleo stepped away from her uncle and wrapped her arms around her middle. What was *he* doing back?

"I see you found the ax handle. I'll get that changed out this afternoon." Uncle Joe rose to slap the carpenter on the back. "Well, Theo, what do you think of my niece going off to New Orleans and becoming a real teacher?"

eighteen

What *did* Theo think of Cleo Trahan going off to New Orleans and becoming a teacher?

Funny, he'd been asking himself that ever since yesterday when he kissed her. Never a day in his life had he ever expected he'd want to be kissing a schoolteacher.

Yet there she stood, the future teacher of the Latagnier school, and all he could think of was kissing her. The very idea made him break out in a sweat.

He wiped his forehead with the back of his hand and forced a grin. "Well, sir, I think that sounds like a fine idea."

But did he?

In a word, no.

A better idea would be to have her stay here, teach the youngsters for a few years, and then. . .what? If he had no designs on her, what did he care whether she went off to that fancy college?

Yet he did care. He cared more than he ever intended to let on, he decided as he listened to Joe rattle on about the school in New Orleans. He cared more about courting her than hearing about the teaching certificate she'd earn.

He'd never admit that to her or anyone else except the Lord, of course. He couldn't.

If he were to say anything about his feelings for that pretty girl, two things would happen. First, he'd probably end up getting hitched to her and never leaving Latagnier. Second, she'd never use the brains God gave her to shape the young folks of the parish.

If either of those things happened, it would be a crying

shame. But the idea of courting Clothilde Trahan did have its merits.

Maybe he'd think on it just a bit.

He turned his gaze on Cleo and saw the happiness on her face as she discussed the teachers' college with her uncle. How could he keep her from what the Lord obviously meant her to do?

What in the world was I thinking? I'm a lot of things, but until now I didn't think one of them was selfish. And to get in the way of a girl's bright future was just plain selfish.

He made a promise right then and there that he'd give Cleo Trahan the only gift he could give her, the gift of her freedom. He of all people knew how precious that gift was.

And he alone would know how hard it was to give.

"Joe, excuse me, but I'm going to head out to the schoolhouse. I know your niece is anxious to get started on her teaching, and I'm itching to hit the road. The quicker I get things finished, the sooner both of us will be happy."

With that, he beat a path out of the kitchen and across the clearing toward the building site. Rather than head directly there, he took a winding path that led him past the bayou. To settle his thinking, he decided.

Without actually thinking, however, he ended up right back at the spot he'd been yesterday. The spot where he'd kissed Cleo.

Settling himself on the log, Theo rested his elbows on his knees and cradled his chin in his hands. He was in quite a fix this time. Maybe there was a way around this, a way where no one would have to give up anything.

Only the Lord knew how he could have his freedom and Cleo Trahan, too. And what of Cleo? Could he bear to take her dreams away from her by asking for her hand in marriage?

He hadn't managed to think of anything else but her ever since he had laid his lips against hers. She fit against him like the Lord had made them together, then broke the mold. And when they kissed, well, the fireworks display he'd watched one year in New York harbor didn't hold a candle to the sparks going off inside his head.

"Lord, *c'est moi*, Theo Breaux. I know You and I don't speak out loud much, but I sure would be obliged if You would make it clear and plain what You want me to do about Cleo."

He waited expectantly, just like the Bible said to do. Any moment the Lord would speak, and then he'd know how to handle the situation. A couple of birds landed on the sweet gum tree across the bayou, and he studied them intently while he waited.

Nothing.

Silence.

"Well, Lord? Are You coming up with anything? I'm plain out of ideas."

Leaning forward, he reached for a stick and began to trace circles in the soft earth. Still nothing from God.

"Lord, are You listening? I need an answer, and I need it now. I've got work to do."

"If only He responded on our time."

Theo whirled around to see Pastor Broussard coming toward him. He dropped the stick and rose to shake the preacher's hand.

"Don't let me disturb you, son," he said. "I was heading for the Trahan place to meet up with Joe and saw you sitting here. I couldn't help but hear your petition to the Lord."

He shrugged. "Well, you might have heard, but I'm not so sure He did."

The pastor chuckled. "It often seems that way, doesn't it? I assure you that His lack of an immediate response doesn't mean He is ignoring you, Theo."

"I know that in my head, but right now my heart's not too keen on the idea." Theo let his shoulders slump. "Truth is, I've got a problem that just about seems to be more than even the Lord can solve."

The pastor's gray brows rose. "My, my, you must have quite a problem if it's worse than spending forty years wandering in the desert unable to find your homeland or sleeping all night in a den of lions." He gave Theo a concerned look. "It doesn't look like Pharaoh's chariots have you backed up to a sea you can't cross."

"No, sir," Theo said.

"And I can't be certain, but I don't believe you've been swallowed by a whale or turned to a pillar of salt lately."

"Can't say as I have."

The Reverend Broussard touched Theo's sleeve. "Then what's so terrible that it's worse than all these calamities?"

Theo took a deep breath and let it out slowly. "Love, sir," he finally said.

"I see." His brows gathered. "Well, you've got me there."

Theo chuckled despite feeling lower than a snake's belly. "You don't know the half of it, Reverend."

"I don't suppose I do," he said, "but I'd be glad to sit a spell with you and listen to your tale of woe. Who knows? I might have a word or two of advice. I *am* a happily married man. Have been for the last thirty-two years."

"What about Joe Trahan. Isn't he expecting you?"

"I reckon Joe'll understand if I'm delayed a bit." He sat on the log and patted the place next to him. "Join me, won't you?"

Theo nodded and settled beside the pastor. "I'd appreciate it if you wouldn't mention to Joe that you spent time with me. I wouldn't want him getting the idea that—"

"That you're mooning over his niece?" He must have looked surprised, for the pastor laughed out loud. "Theo, you're the last one to realize you're crazy in love with her. Some of us figured that out a long time ago."

"Well, I wish someone would have let me in on the secret."

Theo picked up a pebble and tossed it toward the bayou. "I would've lit out of here while I still had a right mind."

The pastor laughed again. "Son, the moment we men take up with the womenfolk, we forfeit any right mind we ever had." He sobered quickly. "But having said that, I will tell you that I love my wife like a silly fool even after all these years, and I wouldn't have it any other way."

"I want that. . .someday."

Rev. Broussard nodded. "Who do you figure is in control here, you or God?"

"God, of course," Theo said.

"Then what are you doing telling Him when you're going to do something? Isn't the issue of timing His concern, not yours?"

"Yes, but He and I have a deal."

The pastor gave Theo a sideways look. "Is that so? What sort of deal?"

"I travel now, and I settle down to a family and responsibilities later."

"Well now, that's quite a nice deal you've worked out with the Lord. Makes me wonder what would have happened if I'd thought to negotiate rather than blindly let Him lead me."

"He *is* leading me. I'm just setting up my life and all those plans for later. You know, after I've seen the world."

Rev. Broussard stood and dusted off the back of his trousers. "Son, have you ever considered the fact that *later* might have already arrived?"

"Maybe so, Reverend, but I'm not the only one who stands to lose here."

"Oh?"

"That's right." He pointed toward the Trahan place. "You know Cleo's got as much to lose as me. More, actually. If she were to marry, there goes her teaching career."

"And you think that's enough to cause her to give up the life God intended for her?"

Theo shrugged. "Depends. What does God want for her? I figure He didn't make her smart like she is just so she can hitch up with a bumpkin like me."

"That's your logic talking, Theo." The pastor laid his hand on Theo's shoulder. "What does your heart say? And more importantly, what does God say?"

"Well now, that's the trouble I was in when you wandered up, Reverend. God's not saying anything, not a word. As for my heart, it's telling me I ought to set her up right with a nice place to teach, then tell her good-bye, and head for the hills. Canada, actually."

"Is that all your heart is telling you?"

What good would it do to lie to a preacher? Not that he was much of a liar anyway. His mama and papa raised him better than that. No, most times it was the truth that got him in trouble and not some fabrication.

"No, sir, it's telling me I'd like to have one more kiss before I go. More if it were proper, which it isn't." If the preacher seemed surprised, he didn't let on. "I'd appreciate it if you'd keep this to yourself, especially that last part."

nineteen

Cleo clutched the broom's handle tightly as she moved the porch rocker and reached to sweep behind it. What was wrong with her this morning?

She should be the happiest girl in Latagnier. Why, then, did she feel as though she'd just heard the worst news of her life?

Uncle Joe had given in. She was going to college to become a teacher. In no time, she'd have a teaching certificate in her hand, and she would be officially able to impart all her knowledge to eager students.

This was her dream, her fervent prayer. Now that the Lord had granted it, why was she so tempted to go to Him and tell Him she'd changed her mind?

After all, Theo Breaux thought it was a good idea, too.

She struck the business end of the broom against the wall to dislodge a spot of dirt, then swept it off the edge of the porch. Watching it land in the bed of Easter lilies, she remembered the carpenter's glee at her uncle's news.

He was downright happy.

The thought irked her and worked irritation into her bones. Couldn't the man have at least indicated he might miss her? After all, there were less than three months left before the fall term.

Three months.

If only Tante Flo were here to talk to. In anticipation of the Easter celebration, coming up in just over a week on April 3, her aunt and some of the other church ladies were busy quilting a new altarpiece. She'd likely spend the whole afternoon at the church.

Of course, Cleo knew she could join them, but sitting with a bunch of married ladies while fretting about a man and her future didn't sound like her idea of a pleasant afternoon.

Not that she'd likely enjoy any activity today.

She swiped at a pebble that had somehow found its way onto the porch, sending it flying into the same bed of lilies. How she'd like to give Theo Breaux a swipe with this broom. Maybe it would knock some sense into him.

A man didn't just kiss a girl, then act like it was a good idea that she leave town. Well, at least not an honorable man.

"My, but this floor does shine."

Cleo jumped and dropped the broom. Rev. Broussard stood on the porch steps, hat in hand.

"Forgive me, dear. I thought you heard me."

Placing her hand over her racing heart, she retrieved the broom. "No, sir, I didn't."

The pastor smiled. "Lost in thought?"

She nodded. "Actually, yes."

"Anything I can help with?" He smiled. "I do have some measure of qualification in the area of giving advice."

Pausing, she considered whether to speak her mind with the pastor and seek his counsel. Before she could decide, she heard her uncle's heavy footsteps coming their way.

"That you, Reverend?" The screen door opened with a squeal, and Uncle Joe stepped out onto the porch. "You ready to go?"

"I am," the pastor said.

"Well, give me just a minute to collect my things, and we can be off." Her uncle turned to face Cleo. "Reverend and I are heading to town. I thought I might mail that letter to New Orleans." He punctuated the statement with a grin, then transferred his attention to the pastor. "Looks like I'm going to have a real live certified, college-educated teacher in the family. Come the fall, Flo and I'll be packing Cleo off to school. How do you feel about that?"

"Well now," Rev. Broussard said. He crossed the distance between them to take Cleo's hand in his. "I think that's a fine honor, Cleo. A real fine honor. We should celebrate."

"Now that *is* a good idea," Uncle Joe said. "I'm going to tell Flo we need to put on a little party for our girl. The Lord blessed us with her and made her smart, and now she's going off to college. I want all of Latagnier to know it."

Cleo mustered a smile in hopes it would match the ones the men wore. Then a thought dawned, and her smile appeared for real. "They haven't accepted me yet, you know. I think we should reserve our celebrations until then." ·

Uncle Joe seemed surprised at her statement. Curiously, the reverend did not.

"Of course they'll accept you, but I see your point." Uncle Joe gestured toward the house. "Yes, well, I'll go fetch my things and we can be off to town, Reverend."

The pastor nodded. "Take your time, Joe. I'll just sit a spell and visit with your niece." He settled on the swing and patted the spot beside him. "Take a break from your sweeping, won't you?"

Cleo looked at the broom handle in her hand and realized she'd forgotten she held it. Propping it against the wall, she sat beside the pastor and heaved a sigh.

"*Quoi y'a?* Something troubling you, child?"

"No, well, *oui*." She curled her fingers around the chain holding the swing, then rested her forehead against the cool metal. "I'm confused, I suppose, and that does trouble me."

"How so, if you don't mind my asking, that is?"

"Oh, I don't mind. I just don't know if I can explain it." She leaned back and listened to the chains clank against one another. "It is all so complicated. I don't know where to begin."

"I suppose this sounds like a cliché, but I always recommend a body begin at the beginning." He patted her shoulder. "Or you don't have to tell me anything. We could merely pray if that will help."

She thought a moment before shaking her head. "Actually, I think it would do me good to talk to someone who could keep my confidence."

He smiled. "Well then, you have the right man for the job. Keeping confidences is what I do best."

Cleo let out another long breath and plunged into her story. "Going to college is exciting. It's amazing to think that an orphan girl from Latagnier could end up going off to college and being a teacher." She turned her gaze to the pastor. "It's what I've always wanted."

"Well, then, why the confusion? Are you afraid, or is there something else bothering you?"

"Afraid? No, I don't think so. I think I am more worried that I've been dreaming the wrong dreams."

"What an interesting way of putting things." He seemed to consider her statement. "I take it you thought you wanted to be a teacher but now you think you're being called to some other occupation. Is that correct?"

Was it? No, not exactly, but how to explain to the reverend without embarrassing herself?

"Occupation isn't quite the word I was thinking of, Rev. Broussard. I guess I'm trying to say I'm not sure if I am being called to an occupation at all."

He looked perplexed. "Then what are you being called to do, child? What is there to do if not work?" Pausing, a smile grew. "Ah, I think I see the dilemma."

"You do?"

The reverend nodded. "Indeed. You thought you were to teach children. Now—and perhaps I'm setting off in a direction you didn't mean to send me—you feel as though the Lord intends you to raise children instead?"

Stunned, she diverted her gaze. She hadn't thought of

things quite that way. A house full of children to raise—and to teach.

Her mind reeled back to daydreams she'd had just days ago, images of dark-haired children with names like Ernest and Angeline. Was that what the Lord wanted of her?

Suddenly her heart lightened. Maybe God gave her the ability to teach so that she could be a better mother and not just so that she might be a better teacher. The idea was no less far-fetched than imagining herself among city folk at the college in New Orleans.

Both had their appeal. And their drawbacks.

Suddenly either one could be her future. Whichever God allowed, she knew she would be happy.

"Cleo?"

She turned her attention to the reverend, who stared at her with a quizzical look. "Yes?"

"That's a nice smile. I haven't seen it for some time. I rather like it."

She broadened her grin. "I like it, too. Thank you, Rev. Broussard."

He placed his hand over his heart and shook his head. "For what? I didn't do a thing." He paused, his face grave. "Cleo, promise me one thing."

"What's that?"

Shifting slightly, he faced her directly. "Promise me that you will wait on a clear direction from the Lord and not depend on your own understanding of what you *think* He would want for you."

Cleo nodded. "I promise. Perhaps I should pray for patience then."

The pastor chuckled. "Oh dear, now that's a dangerous petition to make to the Lord. In my experience, He always seems to grant a request for patience by teaching it to you through experience. In other words, He tends to make you wait."

"Oh my." She joined him in his laughter. "So then, asking for patience is not a good idea. I'll just ask Him to hurry. How's that?"

Rev. Broussard affected a surprised look. "Funny, that's not the first time I've heard that prayer today."

"Oh?"

"Yes, curiously I prayed with a fellow parishioner just before I arrived here. He asked the Lord for the very same thing." The pastor smiled and looked away. "Interesting indeed."

The screen door squealed a warning as it flew open and Uncle Joe spilled out onto the porch. He wore his blue suit and his best hat, and he carried a satchel of papers under his arms. Inside that satchel, Cleo knew, was a letter to New Orleans begging on her behalf for a spot on the fall roster at the college.

He set the satchel on the porch rail and began fumbling through the items inside. "Ah, here it is. Cleo, take a look at this list and see if I've left off any supplies you need for the schoolhouse."

As her gaze ran the length of the page, her mind ticked off the items required for the schoolroom. Each seemed to be present on the list.

"No, I can't think of anything missing," she said as she handed the paper back to her uncle. "It looks like you've thought of everything."

He nodded. "Good. Theo tells me the school will be finished soon. I want everything in place to get started as soon as we can. What with Cleo leaving in a few months, I'd like to get our children into the schoolhouse and learning their lessons as soon as possible."

"I'm not sure the children will be as excited as you, Uncle Joe," Cleo said with a chuckle.

"I have to agree with Cleo," Reverend Broussard said. "But

I do think it will make for a much easier transition once the new teacher arrives if the children are already used to coming to school and tending to their lessons."

Uncle Joe replaced the list in his satchel, then closed the latch. "Theo promised a progress report today. I told him you and I would stop by on our way back from town and see what he's got to show us."

"That sounds like a fine idea," the reverend said as he fell into step beside Uncle Joe.

That sounds like a fine idea. The same words Theo Breaux had used to describe his reaction to Cleo going off to college.

Cleo reached for the broom. What the Lord did with her situation was anyone's guess. What He intended to do with Theo Breaux was another mystery.

At least she knew the one who had the situation in hand. "You know I'd just mess it up if I tried to fix it."

twenty

Theo slipped into church and listened intently as the music swelled around him. He rarely joined the faithful in their singing, choosing to mouth the words rather than ruin the harmony with his squawking.

Today, however, he added his voice to the mix, swept into the words of the song like he'd fallen into the river just ahead of Niagara Falls.

"Oh, what peace we often forfeit. Oh, what needless pain we bear. All because we do not carry everything to God in prayer!"

While the rest of the congregation went on with their singing, Theo stopped right there. He'd been walking around all week shouldering his worries and hadn't even thought to leave them at the cross. That's not true. He'd thought about it; he'd been afraid of the answers he might get if he asked the questions.

Ever since he and the reverend had parted company last Tuesday, he'd been miserable. Worse, every time he took his troubles to the Lord, He said the same thing, so Theo had just quit.

Stay. Be patient.

Stay? Be patient? Stay where? Be patient about what?

Best as he could tell, he'd figured it went like this: He wanted to go—soon—and yet the Lord was telling him he ought to take his time in leaving. He feared God might even be telling him he ought not go at all. Worse, he felt the strongest urge to have a talk with Clothilde Trahan about *her* need to leave Latagnier.

Of course, a logical man would know that none of these things made sense. He'd head for Canada soon, and Cleo, well, she'd be in New Orleans before fall. That's just the way life worked.

Still, he had the nagging feeling the Lord was pushing him in one direction while he stubbornly continued to try to go in another.

Knowing what he wanted to do and what he ought to do were two different things, so Theo elected to do nothing but mope all week. Well, mope and take out his frustrations on several pounds of nails and a good portion of the schoolhouse.

At this rate, he'd be finished with the work out there and ready to hit the road again come the end of April. Maybe sooner.

Rather than let that thought ruin a beautiful Palm Sunday morning, Theo focused on catching up to the rest of the parishioners.

"Jesus knows our every weakness. Take it to the Lord in prayer."

He finished the singing with the rest of the faithful, then sat down between his papa and Alphonse to listen to the preaching. Expecting a message on Jesus' ride on the donkey or some other Palm Sunday topic, he was surprised to hear the Reverend Broussard begin to tell the tale of an itinerant carpenter who made his living working for the less fortunate in Canada.

As the story of songwriter Joseph Scriven unfolded, Theo listened with particular attention. Seemed as though this fellow spent his days doing odd carpentering jobs and taking little or no payment in return. When his mother fell ill back home in Ireland, Scriven wrote her the poem that eventually became the song the congregation had sung that very morning.

"Think on that, ladies and gentlemen," Rev. Broussard said. "Just as the Lord used a lowly animal to carry His

Son on the day we now call Palm Sunday, so He also used a regular man to carry a message that lasts." He paused to lean over the edge of the pulpit and point out into the crowd. "How many of you regular men and women are being called today to do something, and you don't know why? Maybe you don't even want to do it, eh?"

A few murmurs circulated through the room. Beside him, Theo's papa nodded while Theo squirmed.

"Do you think that donkey knew he was carrying the King of glory? Did he know why he was supposed to plod through the city gates with that man on his back, and on his day off at that? And what about that Canadian carpenter? Do you think he knew that a poem he wrote to his ailing mama back home in Ireland was going to be sung in our little church in Latagnier today?"

Again the crowd answered softly or nodded in quiet agreement. Theo saw his mama jab his papa, then watched them share a smile.

"So the next time you think you know what God wants you to do, do it, even if it doesn't make any sense to you. That carpenter, he fixed things for widows and the poor. He wasn't a fancy poet. That donkey, it probably didn't have much claim to glory, either, being as though that particular species of the animal kingdom is not exactly exalted."

Rev. Broussard paused to shake his head. "Brothers and sisters, it all comes down to obedience. Promise yourself that in light of the nature of this upcoming Holy Week, you will settle yourself into a pattern of obedience. Now stand with me while we sing the last verse of that song one more time."

The next time Theo sang about taking his worries to the Lord in prayer, he barely got the words out for the lump in his throat. Knowing he wouldn't like what the Lord was telling him, somewhere midweek he'd stopped going to Him in prayer altogether.

He'd have to remedy that today. This time, he'd listen if the Lord spoke. And as much as it put grit in his craw, he'd obey.

He'd obey even if it killed him.

Funny how he felt he had more in common with the lowly donkey than with the poet-carpenter. While the carpenter knew what he was doing when he wrote that poem, that poor donkey just put one hoof in front of the other and walked all the way to Jerusalem.

Later that afternoon, while the house lay still, Theo slipped away to go back to his thinking spot—the log beside the bayou. There he met the Savior and had a good talk.

It was a one-sided conversation, to be sure, but near the end, when he'd spoken his piece and knelt waiting for a response, Theo felt the Lord's presence.

He hadn't said a word, audible or otherwise, and yet Theo knew He was there. "Sometimes just knowing You're there is enough," he whispered.

Returning home, he felt a renewed spring in his step. While he might have to do something he didn't want to do this week, he at least hadn't been asked to do it yet.

He did have something else in mind, however, something he'd like to do if the Lord and the Reverend Broussard didn't disagree.

❧

Easter Sunday loomed large on Cleo's calendar, circled in red and noted with a star. Now the big day stood just one day away, and she had things to do. Important things.

Over the past week, she'd learned to press past the worries of *when* the Lord would act and *how* He would act and to just be patient and *know* He would act. Of course, this didn't make the waiting any easier, so she'd thrown herself into a flurry of activities.

She'd cooked and washed and starched and ironed. Cleo had even volunteered to go and participate with the quilting circle.

Listening to the married ladies cackle and go on about their husbands and children turned out to be fun. Hearing the love in their voices gave Cleo hope that she would one day have what these women already possessed.

Such was her enthusiasm for keeping busy that today she'd volunteered to clean the entire sanctuary in anticipation for tomorrow's Easter services. She collected her supplies and reached for the bucket's metal handle. Making the church sparkle and shine would be her small contribution to the Lord's Day, and she eagerly anticipated being alone with Jesus in His house as she worked.

Tomorrow would dawn early, with sunrise services being held in the churchyard beside the bayou, then preaching at half past ten in the sanctuary. The entire congregation would break bread together afterward with a spectacular Easter Sunday dinner on the grounds.

Cleo smiled. Easter Sunday had been the same ever since she could remember. Only the pastor's name had changed over the years, and even then there had been only two other preachers besides the Reverend Broussard to grace the pulpit.

There was something to be said for permanence and stability. Some might look at the long and uninterrupted cycle of life in the bayou country and call it boring or backward. Theo Breaux struck her as one of those folks.

Others praised the predictable daily routine as good and comfortable. Cleo wondered if she might better fit in the second category.

Perhaps when she was older, she would know for sure.

Older like Theo Breaux.

She shook off thoughts of the carpenter. Ever since she had her talk with the reverend, she'd placed Theo in a carefully guarded spot in her heart and left him there—at least most days.

But on random occasions, the carpenter managed to sneak

out of his confinement and dance across her mind. Well, not actually dance. When thoughts of him arrived, it was more like the infantry storming through.

Nevertheless, the idea of Theo Breaux dancing did produce a chuckle. She allowed herself that single silly thought, then tucked it away with the others and headed for the church.

Funny how she'd listened to the pastor's sermon and immediately thought of herself. Now, as she passed very near to the place where the carpenter had kissed her, she thought about how Rev. Broussard's words might apply to Theo Breaux.

Here was a man who couldn't read but who had been called on to rebuild a schoolhouse so that others could learn. She knew enough of Theo's history to know he'd left home young and stayed gone until recently, when his papa broke a leg. How difficult it must be for a wandering soul to be confined.

She sighed. "Just another reason why he and I were not meant to be."

Pausing in the middle of the path, she let her feet turn her toward the bayou and the log where she had sat with Theo Breaux. To her surprise, the giant fallen tree trunk was gone.

twenty-one

Cleo looked around to be sure she stood in the correct place. All the landmarks were there: The pine and the sweet gum trees and the honeysuckle vine were all where she remembered them to be.

As she drew nearer, she found a deep indentation in the soft, dark earth where the tree trunk had once landed. This had to be the spot, yet the tree was gone.

Pondering the conundrum all the way to the church, she set her cleaning supplies just outside the door and reached for the massive iron handle. As her fingers wrapped around the cool metal, she heard a strange scratching sound.

Cleo released her grip and followed the sound to the back of the church, where a pile of rope and a hammer sat beside a bag of nails. The scratching sound continued. It seemed to be coming from near the bayou. Pressing through the thicket, she found the source of the noise.

Theo Breaux stood hunched over a large piece of wood while another man held the lumber still. Theo's broad shoulders rolled as he worked a saw across the end of the timber. The other man, whom she recognized as Theo's brother Alphonse, looked up to see her approach but merely nodded and returned his attention to his task.

His back to her, Theo continued to work on chopping off the rough ends of the timber. As Cleo drew near, she realized what the men were doing. Her gasp of surprise seemed to echo louder than the scrape of the saw, although neither man gave notice they'd heard.

The log where just last week she'd sat with Theo now lay

in the clearing in two pieces, one significantly shorter than the other. If she used her imagination, she could see the two planks nailed together to form a cross.

Abruptly the noise ceased, and Theo dropped the saw atop the pile of sawdust. Alphonse grinned and nudged his brother, then pointed toward Cleo.

Theo straightened and turned slowly. His face wore no expression, but his brother's did.

Alphonse's grin split his face, and he looked to be having a hard time keeping from breaking into laughter. "*Bonjour*, Mademoiselle Trahan," he called. "*Comment ça va?* And your family?"

"*Ça va bien, merci,*" she responded. "Thank you for asking."

Cleo turned her attention to Theo but found no words of greeting forthcoming. He obviously had the same trouble, for he merely nodded, then went back to his work.

Alphonse said something to his brother and bounded toward her. "So what brings you out to the church today?"

"Cleaning the sanctuary."

She looked past him to where Theo now rubbed a metal file against the edge of the freshly cut wood. The dark fabric of his shirt bunched and stretched as he worked his powerful arms to move the tool across the rough timber.

Remembering the feel of those arms around her, heat flooded Cleo's cheeks. Perhaps the fact that this man was the roaming kind was a blessing. He might never completely leave her mind, but at least she wouldn't have his presence to distract her.

Not that she minded the distraction.

"Fine day, isn't it?"

"What?" She forced her attention back to Alphonse Breaux. "I'm sorry. What did you say?"

Theo's brother gave her a good-natured grin, then shook his head. A sprinkling of wood shavings fell from his dark hair. From a distance, the two men could practically be mistaken for twins. Up close, however, the younger Breaux had none of his older brother's careworn demeanor.

Where Theo's eyes had creases at the corner, Alphonse's were wide and unmarred by time and worry. His forehead held no lines, and his square jaw bore none of the perpetual stubble like his brother's.

In a word, Alphonse Breaux was the very definition of handsome. All the girls at church thought so, and he never lacked for female companionship.

Funny, but Cleo preferred to cast her gaze on the less-perfect Theo instead.

"I was commenting on the weather. Making small talk. Never mind."

"That's nice." Her gaze swept across the landscape, from the two timbers, to Theo, and finally rested on Alphonse. "What are you doing?"

He shrugged. "Can't tell you. Actually I don't think you're supposed to be out here. Theo wanted this to be a surprise."

"Oh." She cast a quick glance at Theo, who seemed to be hard at work. "Well, I promise not to tell what I've seen. Not that I know what I'm looking at."

"That's good. I'm sure Theo will appreciate that." Alphonse swiped at his forehead, then studied the back of his hand. "You know, Mademoiselle Trahan, I'm puzzled by something. Maybe you can help me with it."

Theo glanced over his shoulder, then returned to his work as if he hadn't noticed she still stood nearby. Well, two could play at this game.

"What are you confused about, Alphonse?"

"Here's how I see it. I hear tell you're going to teach at the schoolhouse until fall and then you're heading for school out in New Orleans. Is that right?"

A brisk wind blew past, and she brushed a strand of hair from her eyes. "Yes, that's right."

"And Theo over there, he's chomping at the bit to get the schoolhouse finished so he can get himself up to Canada to see the first snowfall."

"That's what I hear."

Alphonse nodded and seemed to be considering his thoughts carefully. His brow creased, and he shook his head. "So if you want to head off to school and Theo wants to head off to Canada, and you are both getting what you want, what's the problem?"

Cleo shrugged. "I don't guess there is a problem."

Again, Theo's brother nodded. "I see. Well, that's funny, because I don't remember when I've ever seen my brother look more miserable, and truth be told, you're not exactly smiling real big today, either."

To prove him wrong, she forced a grin. It only lasted a moment.

"You and my brother, I think you have something special. *Sa fini pas.* The thing that never ends."

Sa fini pas. Interesting. But then, hadn't she just had the same thought, that he might be leaving, but he'd never completely be gone?

"Forgive me, Mademoiselle Trahan, but I think you and Theo are both stubborn as mules. Neither one of you wants to admit that you've made the wrong plans."

How could someone so handsome say something so rude and get away with it? Because it was true.

"Alphonse! *Vien ici.* Quit your flirting and get back over here. There's work to be done."

Alphonse waved to his brother and turned to trot away. "I'm doing your job over here, and now you want me to do it over there, too?" He glanced back at Cleo and winked. "He's going to get me for that as soon as you leave. When you see me bruised and bandaged, remember I did it for you, Mademoiselle Trahan."

"Enough, Alphonse," Theo called. "I'm sure the lady's got better things to do than to listen to you talk nonsense."

"Yes, well, I'll just get back to work myself then," she said, but neither brother responded. They were too busy circling one another like tomcats.

❧

All afternoon, Cleo listened to mysterious clangs and bangs and other assorted sounds coming from the vicinity of the Breaux brothers' work area.

At one point, Alphonse left for a spell, then returned with shovels—two of them. He winked at her when he spied her peeking out the window. She backed up quickly and pretended to busy herself with dusting, just in case he decided to come inside to say hello.

He didn't, however, and neither did Theo.

Upon finishing the dusting, Cleo decided it was time to take a short rest—just a few minutes of repose before she tackled the job of polishing the candlesticks.

Casually stepping into the afternoon sun, Cleo stretched and sat, then stood and headed for the bayou. Whatever those two were up to out there, she intended to find out.

Getting close to the bayou was the hard part, for she had to go all the way around the church and the cemetery to avoid walking through the clearing. By the time she reached her destination, her ankles had tangled with enough thorns to mark her permanently.

Once she found her way into the thicket, she had to shift positions until she could make out the work site. To do this, she had to lie flat and crawl beneath a tangle of honeysuckle vines, not a feat she could manage easily but one she thought she could accomplish all the same.

Her apron got caught several times, and more than once she had to stop and remove clods of dirt and leaves from the pockets. Finally she untied it and tossed it aside, giving thanks that she'd taken on the job of the Trahan family laundry several years ago.

Eventually she managed to make her way across the distance to find a spot where she could sit comfortably. From her vantage point, she could make out a mass of wood and one man working on it. Both Theo and Alphonse wore dark shirts and trousers, so it was impossible to tell who did the work.

It was also impossible to tell what sort of work was being done, so she inched forward and peered through the vines. Noting a natural clearing a few feet ahead, she decided to try and make her way toward it.

As she leaned forward, she found she could not move her right ankle. From her prone position, she couldn't tell what had happened, but it felt for all the world as if something held her in its grasp. With the thickness of the vines obscuring her view, she couldn't see a thing.

The harder she pulled, the more she seemed to be stuck. Finally, she realized she had to turn around and go back the way she came. This would be the only way to free herself.

Rolling over, she sat up and began to pull the vines apart with her hands. As the dark green leaves fell away, she saw the reason for her troubles.

Theo Breaux sat on the other side of the honeysuckle vine, her apron in one hand and her foot firmly in the other.

"Looking for your apron?"

When he released her foot, she scrambled out of the thicket. Climbing to her feet, Cleo shook the leaves from her dress and hair and reached for her apron. The carpenter stepped back and held the formerly white cloth to his chest.

"Not so fast," he said. "You were spying again."

Her dignity and her apron in shreds, Cleo didn't bother to deny his claim. She held out her hand and waited for him to place the apron in it. When he did, she ran all the way back to the church, his laughter chasing her inside.

With anger and humiliation fueling her, Cleo made short order of the rest of her cleaning, then headed home. On her way, she felt the temptation to stop by the schoolhouse. After all, with Theo at the church, there was no better time to visit.

Reaching the bend in the path, she elected to go home instead. Whatever awaited at the school, it would still be there on Monday. Tante Flo would need her to help with the cooking for tomorrow, and Uncle Joe would most likely have her school supplies.

More to the point, the schoolhouse reminded her of Theo Breaux, and his was a memory she didn't want to think about right now. Maybe not ever.

Still, as she made tracks for home, something about him gave her pause. She knew how she felt about the man, but had she ever asked the Lord His opinion?

twenty-two

The Easter Sunday sunrise was still a good hour away when Cleo and her aunt and uncle climbed into the wagon and headed to church. Tante Flo had the back packed with enough food to feed an army, and still she fretted about whether she'd made enough.

When they arrived at the church, they found a crowd had already begun to gather inside the sanctuary. Cleo noticed the sizable Breaux family carrying on boisterous conversations among themselves over on the left-hand side of the sanctuary, so she turned to head the other way. While she busied herself helping Tante Flo and the other ladies, she kept watch over the doors in case Theo Breaux were to walk in.

Pastor Broussard and his wife greeted the visitors and moved about between the groups of families until he finally climbed to the platform to stand behind the pulpit. As was his custom, Theo slipped inside just as the preacher began to speak.

"It figures," she said as she watched him disappear into a crowd of Breaux family members. This time, however, she spoke the words gently and with humor.

"What figures, dear?" Tante Flo asked.

"Nothing," she said softly, avoiding her aunt's direct gaze. "Listen, the pastor's about to speak."

"Good men and women, let me wish you all the most blessed of Easter Sundays." He paused to allow the parishioners to add their own greetings to one another. "This year our sunrise service will be a little different. A pair of our members have prepared a surprise for us that I believe you all will like very much."

He gestured toward the back exit. "If you will all follow our elders, we will make our way outside and begin our worship."

Cleo filed out with the rest of the congregation, then stood beside Tante Flo until the pastor and his wife emerged from the church. "I wonder what this is about," she whispered to her aunt.

Tante Flo shrugged. "You never can tell," she said softly. "Let's find your uncle."

They spotted Uncle Joe and made their way through the crowd to reach his side. "Do you know what this is about, Joe?" her aunt asked.

Rather than answer, Uncle Joe put his finger over his lips and pointed toward the pastor.

"Folks, I'd like us all to begin now with a song. Rather than stand out here as is our custom, we'll be heading down to the bayou. The path's been lit up, and it should be quite safe. Still, mothers may want to watch the little ones as we all walk together."

He nodded to his wife. "Berta will begin the singing, and we'll all fall in behind her."

As the elderly soprano began the first line of "Amazing Grace," the crowd joined in. Soon the group turned the corner of the church and headed across the clearing toward the bayou.

At the edge of the path, a lantern hung from a tree limb, providing just enough light to see. The same had been done at intervals, each lantern shining a circle of light that enabled the church members to walk in safety.

Cleo held tight to her aunt's arm, noting with wonder the way the deep blue of the night sky was gradually giving way to the gray of morning. By the time she reached the bayou, the tiniest sliver of orange showed on the horizon.

In degrees, the landscape began to emerge, becoming more visible as the sun tried harder to rise. By the time the song ended, most of the church folk had gathered. Cleo looked past them to watch the bayou flow by, an endless river of black punctuated by green on both sides.

The Reverend Broussard cleared his throat. "Let us pray."

As the pastor gave thanks for the day and for the Savior who died and rose for them, Cleo let her own prayers mingle with his. When the *amen*s were said, she opened her eyes to see that the elders of the church had retrieved the lanterns.

Five men walked single file toward the bayou, passing the crowd to stop at the edge of the trees. As the men gathered together, the light from the lanterns illuminated an amazing sight.

Behind them a massive wooden cross rose almost to the treetops. "Let us sing," the pastor said.

As the congregation's voices mingled in song, Cleo's gaze scanned the crowd for signs of Theo Breaux. She found him standing apart from the gathering, leaning against the trunk of a pine tree.

Any other time she would have let the ornery man be, but this morning something drew her to him. Making her way through the friends and relatives took some doing, but Cleo managed to reach his side before the preaching began.

"It's beautiful," she said.

The orange sky glinted off his dark hair and gave his face a golden glow, while the dim light cast half his features in shadow. Rather than the frown she expected, he gave her a wry smile.

"Yes, for once I would have to agree with you, *cher.*"

❧

And Theo did agree. Cleo was beautiful. Too beautiful. That made forgetting her all the more difficult.

He was no saint, even though he really wanted to be. He'd seen pretty women in his time, but not one of them held a candle to this simple bayou beauty.

As the pastor settled into his stride and began regaling the crowd with the finer points of the resurrection story, Theo allowed his attention to drift from the reverend to the cross and finally to the woman who still stood at his side. The thought occurred to him that ever since he had met Cleo, he'd been plotting on how best to remember her—and how to forget her.

What the Lord had in mind when He set her in Theo's line of sight, he'd never know. Still Theo closed his eyes and gave thanks that the Lord had set her there all the same.

If only He weren't continuing to remain silent on what to do about her. *Lord, if You wouldn't mind meeting me here on this Easter Sunday morning, I'd sure like some sign of what You're up to.*

He opened his eyes and gazed on the cross he and Alphonse had set into the ground late last night. Even though he'd cut and planed the wood himself, with his brother's help, nothing prepared him for the sight of it standing this morning.

Somewhere between the closing hymn and the benediction, Cleo slipped her hand into his. He leaned down to protest, only to have her kiss him full on the mouth.

His shock must have shown, for he could only stand mute as she gave him a smile and slipped off into the crowd. As he looked around to see if there were any witnesses to Cleo's kiss-and-run, he noted with dismay that there had been at least one: his papa.

Their gazes met, and Theo knew his goose was cooked. Once the service ended, Papa would certainly have something to say about what he'd seen. As he expected, when the congregation began to mill about, Papa hobbled toward him and poked him with his cane.

"How about you and me speaking privately, Son?" He gestured toward the bayou. "Let's walk that way."

Theo followed his father away from the crowd, staying close enough to catch him should he fall. To his relief, his father had regained his agility. Unfortunately, that same agility got them to their conversation much too soon.

Papa eased himself down on a tree stump and gestured for Theo to sit, as well. When Theo complied, his father leaned forward and regarded him with a serious look.

"You want to tell me the whole story right up front, or am I going to have to ask you a bunch of questions and drag it out of you?"

Theo sighed. "I guess I ought to just start at the beginning and lay it all out."

As his father nodded, Theo began his tale. When he got to the part about asking the Lord not to let him miss out on life like his father had, he saw Papa wince. Pressing on, he finished his story, then leaned back against the pine tree and waited for the reaction.

When Papa leaned on his cane and stared down at Theo, he figured the time for a lecture had arrived. And then Papa laughed. Right there on Easter Sunday morning, his father had listened to Theo tell him he didn't want to end up in the same situation as he was in, and he responded by laughing.

"I'm sorry, Son," Papa said. "But I think you've got it all wrong here. I didn't miss a thing."

"But you could've gone to college, made something of yourself." Theo cringed. "I'm sorry, I didn't mean to say that. . . ."

Papa waved away the statement with a swipe of his cane. "Yes, you did, but that's all right. I'd think that, too, if I didn't know better." He shrugged. "After all, what the world looks on as success isn't always all it's cracked up to be."

Theo shook his head. "I know, but don't you ever wonder what it would have been like if you'd gone to Texas and earned your diploma at the college? I mean, you'd certainly not have ended up here in Latagnier."

He nodded. "Well, you're right about that, Son, which is exactly why I believe you miss the point."

"I don't understand."

"You asked me if I ever wonder what I missed by staying

here. I don't, but let me tell you what I do wonder sometimes. I wonder what it would be like if I'd set off to seek my fortune and missed out on nigh on thirty years of marriage with the love of my life."

The sounds of churchgoers buzzed in the distance as Theo thought about his father's statement. "I suppose I see your point," he said. "But look at you. You're up before the sun, work your fingers until they bleed, then fall into bed at night dead tired. The next morning you do it all over again. I don't want that life. No, not me."

Papa looked away and closed his eyes. "Is that what you see when you look at me? Do you really think that's all there is to my life?"

Theo thought a minute, then shook his head. In reality, when he considered his papa, work was the last thing that came to mind. His quick wit, his endless patience, and his ability to endure without losing his love for the Lord—those were the things he thought of.

Above all these, however, Theo knew he would remember his father for the way he openly and eternally showed how much he loved his wife and children.

"No, sir. I don't suppose I do." He repeated his thoughts to his father, then shared a grin with him. "So what do you make of Cleo Trahan?"

"Other than the fact that she has excellent taste in men?"

If Theo knew how to blush, he would have done it at that moment. Instead he shrugged. "Runs in the family, I guess."

Papa nodded. "But my guess is, you're not sure she's the one."

"Well. . ." He struggled to answer his father.

"The fact you can't agree tells me a whole lot."

Theo slapped his knees. "I'm not sure what to do, Papa. If I admit I care for her, I risk giving up my freedom. At the same time, she'd be giving up her teaching. What marriage can survive that?"

Papa rose slowly and waited for Theo to join him. "You ask what marriage can survive? Look at your mama and me. We buried two babies before they could walk and stared each other down in head-to-head disagreements more times than a gator has scales. I'm as hardheaded as a mule, and I snore louder than a brass band on Independence Day. On top of that, and I know you'll find this difficult to believe, I tend to be set in my ways and don't like to admit I'm wrong. Know anybody like that?"

Theo dusted off the seat of his pants and met his father's gaze. "No, can't say as I do." He shrugged. "You can't be comparing yourself to me. I don't snore."

The pair shared a laugh, then walked back to the gathering together. Just before they rejoined the group, Papa laid his hand on Theo's shoulder and pulled him aside.

"Son, don't make the mistake of deciding what God's will is for that girl. You worry about what He wants you to do, and He'll take care of the rest."

"Yes, sir." He took a step toward the clearing, but his father held him back.

"And Theo, you need to realize that what you think you're missing isn't out there. It's right here." He thumped Theo on the chest. "You get your heart right with God, and He takes care of your need to find happiness anywhere else."

"As for the adventure you think you're looking for. . ." He pointed to the group of women where Cleo stood. "I'd wager a week's wages and my good leg that it's right over there."

The object of their discussion met his gaze. She offered a smile, then a discreet wave. He nodded and turned his attention to his father. "Anything else, Papa?"

Papa nodded and motioned for him to lean close. "Just one more thing."

"All right."

"You *do* snore."

twenty-three

"It's Sunday evening," Uncle Joe called. "Who in the world would be calling on a body on Easter Sunday? Why, we've already talked to just about everyone in the parish this morning at church."

"Hush, Joe," Tante Flo said. "That's not neighborly at all. Cleo, would you see who is at the door?"

"Oui."

Cleo rose from her spot on the settee, leaving her book open so she could easily rejoin the adventure unfolding on the pages. To her surprise, she opened the door to find Theo Breaux standing there. Dressed in his Sunday best, he'd taken the unprecedented step of slicking his unruly hair back in a style vaguely resembling the latest fashion.

"Bonsoir, Cleo. Is your uncle home?" He thrust a motley collection of spring flowers in her direction.

Cleo suppressed a giggle. "Why? Are those for him?"

He seemed a bit disconcerted. "No, they're for you."

"Who's there, Cleo?" Uncle Joe called.

"It's your carpenter," she said as she stepped back and ushered him inside.

He and Joe shook hands, then Theo cleared his throat. "I'd like to speak to you in private, sir."

Uncle Joe looked up at Theo over the rim of his spectacles. "Would you now?"

The pair went into the kitchen. When Cleo tiptoed toward the closed door, her aunt stepped out to touch her shoulder. She jumped and whirled around.

"Go and read your book, child, while I put these in some

water," Tante Flo said as she took the flowers from Cleo. "For once in our life, let the menfolk be."

Somehow she managed to settle back onto the settee and pick up the book. Reading, however, was out of the question, as her mind kept reeling back in time to the morning's sunrise service.

Had she really stolen a kiss during church? Why, she'd behaved no better than. . .than what? She blushed to think of the comparison she could make.

Abruptly the kitchen door flew open, and Theo emerged, followed by Uncle Joe. Without a word, the carpenter took Cleo by the hand.

"Let's go for a walk," he said as he led her toward the door.

She cast a glance over her shoulder in time to see Uncle Joe disappear down the hall. Obviously, whatever transpired in the kitchen, her uncle was neither excited nor upset about it.

Following Theo outside, she paused to suppress a chill. When had the air grown so cold?

Before she could turn and fetch her shawl, Theo removed his suit coat and draped it over her shoulders. The heavy wool felt heavenly against her shoulders as she snuggled into its warmth.

They walked along in silence for a time, and Cleo marveled at how comfortable it felt. When Theo cleared his throat, she almost jumped.

"You're probably wondering why I showed up here tonight." He gestured toward his clothes. "Dressed like this."

Cleo met his gaze, then allowed her attention to slide lower to his neck. A vein pulsed there, and she wondered if his heart raced as fast.

"Actually, I did wonder." She paused to add the beginning of a smile. "A bit, anyway."

He guided her toward the bayou, falling in step beside her. "I'm not sure where to start, so I guess I'll just tell you right out." He shook his head. "No, I don't think I'll do it that way. I believe I'll just show you."

Grasping Cleo's hand, he picked up his pace. She nearly had to run to keep up with his long strides. By the time they reached the schoolhouse, she was out of breath.

Theo slowed his pace when he saw her distress. "I'm really sorry, Cleo," he said. "Why didn't you say something?"

She shrugged. "We're here now," she managed. "What was it you wanted to show me?"

He climbed up on the porch, then gestured for her to follow. At the door, he stepped back and pointed to the handle. "You do the honors, Cleo. It's your schoolhouse."

Cleo gave him a long look before opening the door and stepping inside. The first thing that she noticed was the smell. Everything smelled fresh and clean and—and new.

Theo rushed to the windows and began raising the shades. As light flooded the room, Cleo shook her head. It was finished.

Her gaze flitted from desk to bench to chalkboard and back to Theo. Somewhere along the way, tears had begun to fall. Theo raced to her side.

"*Quoi y'a, cher?* What is it? Have I done something wrong?"

"Wrong? No. *Pas du tout.* It's. . .it's perfect."

She glanced around the room once more. True to his word, Theo Breaux had turned the little ramshackle building into something resembling a proper schoolhouse.

Sturdy wooden benches sat in three straight rows on the patched cypress floor, providing room enough for nearly a dozen children to sit. Three windows on either side of the room allowed a breeze to float across the little room. Cleo closed her eyes, imagining the bright faces of children eager to learn, then opened them once more to see Theo staring.

To her surprise, his eyes seemed to be watering. Or was that a tear?

"Theo, are you all right?"

Nodding, he grasped her hand and brought her fingers to touch his lips. "It's just that I'm going to miss you."

She kissed his fingers, then fell into his arms. "Are you asking me to stay?"

Pressing her ear to his chest, she could hear his heart racing. "I can't ask that of you," he said.

The words rumbled through her heart and lodged in her throat. "Can't or won't?"

He released his grip to hold her at arm's length. "I won't be the reason your dreams don't come true, Cleo."

She stared into the eyes of the orneriest man in Latagnier and gave passing thought to what life might be like without him. "Just as I refuse to be the reason yours don't come true. Tell me I'm worth giving up your traveling ways."

She knew from his expression that she'd hit a nerve. "I'm not, am I?"

His silence spoke volumes. Shrugging out of Theo's jacket, she threw it in his direction and fled for the safety of home.

"Leave me be," she shouted when he tried to follow her. "And don't come around me until you're ready to say I'm more important to you than some trip north. I don't want to love you only to end up with a broken heart, so if you're going, go now."

When he froze in his tracks, her heart broke for real.

❧

The first week of school flew by, as did the second and third. Sometime during the fourth week, Cleo got wind through one of the church ladies that Theo Breaux had left Latagnier on the evening train two weeks back. He was heading north, she'd been told. Canada was what his brother claimed.

Cleo listened to the reports, then went back to her quilting. Her tears would wait for bedtime. They always did.

Berta Broussard met her gaze and changed the subject.

Before long, the ladies had moved on to jawing about the rising cost of thread in town and the prospect of a fall festival to raise money for new candlesticks in the sanctuary.

When Uncle Joe interrupted the party, Cleo was almost relieved. "I'm sorry, ladies, but Cleo is needed at the schoolhouse."

"Really?" She gathered her scissors and thimble and dropped them into her bag. "Is there something wrong?"

After all, today was Saturday. No one should be at the school.

"I think you'd better see for yourself," he said. "But don't tarry."

Cleo rushed toward the school, her gaze scanning the treetops for some sign of smoke or other calamity. When she reached the clearing, relief flooded her. Whatever was wrong, at least the place hadn't gone up in flames.

In fact, the building looked the same today as she had left it after school yesterday. Easing her way up the steps, she tiptoed across the porch to push open the door.

She stepped inside and glanced around. Everything looked to be in order.

Venturing further, she noted the books still lined up on the desks and the pencils and paper neatly stacked on the shelf beneath a chart showing the consonants and vowels. A sound behind her made her jump.

She turned in time to see a tall shadow cross the floor.

"Theo?" A dozen different emotions assailed her, each giving way to the next until she'd lost any idea of how she felt about seeing the carpenter again.

He nodded. "Am I still welcome here?"

For a moment she had no answer. Slowly, she nodded. "Of course," she said. "This schoolhouse belongs to everyone who lives in Latagnier."

As soon as she said the words, she longed to reel them back

in. Theo Breaux no longer lived in Latagnier. Or did he?

He crossed the distance between them in long strides and came close enough to take her in his arms. Close enough, yet he just stood there, arms at his sides, staring.

"Why did you come back?"

More words she wished she hadn't said.

"Something you said. I had to see if you meant it."

"Something I said?" She'd said plenty that day, most of it not so nice.

He nodded. "You said you didn't want to be responsible for my dreams not coming true. Did you mean that?"

It was her turn to nod. Their gazes collided. The impact rocked her to her toes.

"Yes, I meant it," she whispered.

Theo took her hand in his. "Well, I had to get halfway to Canada before I figured out you were the reason my dreams weren't coming true."

"I don't understand."

Theo went down on one knee and kissed her hand. "Without you, I don't have any dreams. I can't imagine life without you in it, and I can't see spending our days anywhere but right here in Latagnier. What I'm saying is I had to learn the hard way that here is where I belong, and you belong right by my side. *Je t'aime*—Oh, how I love you, Cleo Trahan. Will you marry me?"

Words gathered in her mind but stuck in her throat. Somehow she managed to say just one: "Yes."

His expression turned serious. "You'd better think before you answer, Cleo. Setting your sites on being the future Mrs. Breaux will mean you have to give up going to that fancy teachers' college."

She smiled. "I don't give a fig about that school." Sobering a moment, she regarded Theo. "But I wonder what Uncle Joe will think."

"Uncle Joe's fine with the idea." She looked up to see her uncle standing in the door. Tante Flo was beside him. "Has she said yes yet?"

"He knew?" Cleo looked down at the carpenter in astonishment. "How did you get my uncle involved in this?"

"Remember the day I came to the house with flowers?"

She nodded.

"And the conversation in the kitchen? The one you tried to eavesdrop on?"

Again she nodded.

"I told him then that I aimed to marry up with you as soon as I came to my senses."

"Took you long enough, boy," Uncle Joe said.

"Well, Cleo, are you willing to take on an old fool like me?"

She pretended to consider the question. "How many babies do you want, Theo?"

He seemed surprised. "As many as you and the Lord will allow."

"I like this man," Tante Flo said.

"I do, too," Cleo said.

And with that, Theo rose to kiss his future bride.

epilogue

Cleo stood in front of the parlor's rosewood-framed mirror and endured her aunt's scrutiny yet again. The wedding dress was already perfect, and still Tante Flo insisted on one more fitting, one more pin here, one more tuck there.

"Please, Tante Flo, can't we be done with it?" A knock at the door halted Cleo's protest. "I'll get that."

Her aunt stood between her and the door. "Oh no, you don't. What if it's Theo? You know he's not supposed to see you in your wedding dress before the wedding."

"That's a silly superstition designed to keep the groom from running away out of sheer terror. The wedding's tomorrow," she said, yet she allowed her aunt to trot to the front door.

Fretting with a pin, she nearly poked herself when she heard her aunt screech. "Stop right there, Theo Breaux. You cannot go in there. Your bride is in her wedding dress."

Theo's deep voice rumbled a protest. A moment later, Tante Flo returned to the parlor, flustered.

"That man is quite the charmer. I do believe he could sell ice to an Eskimo." She bustled about the room, pulling her best lace tablecloth out of the sideboard. "Here, cover yourself with this. If I let that man in here, I don't want him to be able to see your dress."

Cleo complied, then leaned toward her aunt. "Did he kiss you, too? That's how he manages to charm me."

Her aunt blushed beet red. "Of course not. Now don't be silly. And none of those kisses until tomorrow after the wedding."

Theo peered around the door. "Can I come in now?"

When Tante Flo gave her permission, the carpenter sauntered into the room. Cleo immediately claimed a contraband kiss. Then, before she would let him explain the brown paper package under his arm, she had to steal just one more.

"Someday you're going to get tired of my kisses," Theo said.

"Never," she responded as she patted the place next to her on the settee.

"What are you wearing?"

"Great-grandmother Trahan's Irish lace tablecloth. Do you like it? It's the height of fashion. Everyone wears them over their wedding dresses nowadays."

Theo looked her up and down, then smiled. "On you it looks good," he responded.

For saying just the right thing, she stole yet another kiss. This one lingered a bit longer than the others.

"If I weren't marrying you tomorrow, I'd probably need to be rushing you to the preacher tonight," he said softly. When she leaned in for yet another kiss, he shook his head. "I need to give you this present, Cleo, and if you don't stop that, I'm going to forget what I planned to say."

Smiling, she leaned away. "Go ahead and make your speech then."

He nodded. "I'd like you to have this, Cleo. Go ahead and open it."

She accepted the package, then pulled the string to let the paper fall away. Inside she found a beautiful, leather-bound Bible. Someone had written their names and the next day's date on the page reserved for family weddings.

"Theo, this is. . ." Words failed her. "Thank you."

Her groom-to-be smiled and pointed to the handwriting. "Did I do it right?"

"Do what right?" She traced the names with her index finger. "Oh, Theo, did you write this?"

"Yes," he said softly. "Alphonse showed me how. Is it right?"

"It's perfect." The image before her swirled and disappeared as tears collected in her eyes. "Simply perfect."

"I need to ask you something, Cleo. Something real important."

"What?"

He laid his hand over the Bible. "I want to be able to read this book, Cleo. It's important to me. I want to read it for myself and. . ." He paused and seemed to have difficulty continuing. "And I want to read it to our children. I want to be the head of our house and the godly papa our children deserve, and I'm going to have to call on the words in here to be able to do that. Will you teach me to read, *cher*?"

She cradled his chin in her hand, feeling the rough skin graze her palm. And the bride said, "I will."

CLEO TRAHAN'S SHRIMP ÉTOUFFÉE

- 4 cups butter
- 2 cups each chopped onions, bell peppers, celery, and parsley
- ¼ cup green onions
- 1 clove garlic, chopped
- 2 teaspoons salt
- ½ teaspoon black pepper
- ½ teaspoon cayenne pepper
- 2 tablespoons flour
- 2–3 pounds peeled shrimp (medium to small)
- 2 cups water

Melt butter over medium heat, then sauté vegetables until tender, adding the garlic for the last 2–3 minutes of cooking time (10–15 total minutes). Add salt, black and red peppers, and shrimp and stir until shrimp turn pink (around 5 minutes depending on size of shrimp). In a separate bowl, stir together flour and water until the mixture thickens and resembles a thin gravy. Add flour mixture to shrimp and vegetables and stir until the gravy thickens to the desired consistency (5–10 minutes), then turn heat to low and simmer uncovered for 10 minutes. Stir in parsley and green onions, reserving a small amount to use as garnish, and cook another 2–3 minutes. Serve over white rice with parsley and green onion garnish. Feeds 4–6 hungry Cajuns.

TANTE FLO'S LATAGNIER *GATEAU DE SIROP* WITH CINNAMON PECAN TOPPING

Cake:

    1 cup solid vegetable shortening
    1 cup sugar
    1 cup pure cane syrup
    1 cup boiling water
    1 egg
    ½ teaspoon baking powder
    1 teaspoon each cinnamon, nutmeg, and salt
    ½ teaspoon baking soda
    1½ cups flour

Topping:

    ½ cup light brown sugar
    2½ teaspoons cinnamon
    1 teaspoon nutmeg
    3 tablespoons flour
    3 tablespoons butter (not margarine)
    ½ cup chopped pecans (optional)

Cake:

Grease and flour a 9" cake pan and set aside. In a large mixing bowl, cream together shortening, sugar, and syrup, then add water and stir thoroughly. Beat egg and add to mixture, blending well. In a separate bowl, mix spices, baking soda, and flour then add to cake mixture. Beat until smooth and creamy. Pour into cake pan and bake 30–35 minutes in a preheated 350-degree oven. Cake is done when it shrinks away from the edges of the pan. Remove from oven and set aside for 5–10 minutes while topping is prepared.

Topping:

While cake is cooling, mix together all the ingredients for topping. Spread onto slightly cooled cake and return to oven to bake until topping melts (10–12 minutes). Makes one 9-inch cake.

A Letter To Our Readers

Dear Reader:

In order that we might better contribute to your reading enjoyment, we would appreciate your taking a few minutes to respond to the following questions. We welcome your comments and read each form and letter we receive. When completed, please return to the following:

Fiction Editor
Heartsong Presents
PO Box 719
Uhrichsville, Ohio 44683

1. Did you enjoy reading *Bayou Beginnings* by Kathleen Miller Y'Barbo?
   ❑ Very much! I would like to see more books by this author!
   ❑ Moderately. I would have enjoyed it more if

   _____

   _____

   _____

2. Are you a member of **Heartsong Presents**? ❑ Yes ❑ No
   If no, where did you purchase this book? _____

   _____

3. How would you rate, on a scale from 1 (poor) to 5 (superior), the cover design? _____

4. On a scale from 1 (poor) to 10 (superior), please rate the following elements.

   ____ Heroine   ____ Plot
   ____ Hero   ____ Inspirational theme
   ____ Setting   ____ Secondary characters

5. These characters were special because? _____

_____

_____

6. How has this book inspired your life? _____

_____

_____

7. What settings would you like to see covered in future
   Heartsong Presents books? _____

_____

_____

8. What are some inspirational themes you would like to see
   treated in future books? _____

_____

_____

9. Would you be interested in reading other **Heartsong
   Presents** titles? ❑ Yes ❑ No

10. Please check your age range:
     ❑ Under 18   ❑ 18-24
     ❑ 25-34   ❑ 35-45
     ❑ 46-55   ❑ Over 55

Name _____

Occupation _____

Address _____

City, State, Zip _____

Schoolhouse Brides

4 stories in 1

The lives of four schoolmarms are complicated by unexpected encounters. Can these women find a place in their hearts for love? Titles by authors Wanda E. Brunstetter, JoAnn A. Grote, Yvonne Lehman, and Colleen L. Reece.

Contemporary, paperback, 352 pages, 5³/₁₆" x 8"

Heart♥ng

HEARTSONG PRESENTS TITLES AVAILABLE NOW:

___HP352	*After the Flowers Fade*, A. Rognlie	___HP460	*Sweet Spring*, M. H. Flinkman
___HP356	*Texas Lady*, D. W. Smith	___HP463	*Crane's Bride*, L. Ford
___HP363	*Rebellious Heart*, R. Druten	___HP464	*The Train Stops Here*, G. Sattler
___HP371	*Storm*, D. L. Christner	___HP467	*Hidden Treasures*, J. Odell
___HP372	*'Til We Meet Again*, P. Griffin	___HP468	*Tarah's Lessons*, T. V. Bateman
___HP380	*Neither Bond Nor Free*, N. C. Pykare	___HP471	*One Man's Honor*, L. A. Coleman
___HP384	*Texas Angel*, D. W. Smith	___HP472	*The Sheriff and the Outlaw*,
___HP387	*Grant Me Mercy*, J. Stengl		K. Comeaux
___HP388	*Lessons in Love*, N. Lavo	___HP475	*Bittersweet Bride*, D. Hunter
___HP392	*Healing Sarah's Heart*,	___HP476	*Hold on My Heart*, J. A. Grote
	T. Shuttlesworth	___HP479	*Cross My Heart*, C. Cox
___HP395	*To Love a Stranger*, C. Coble	___HP480	*Sonoran Star*, N. J. Farrier
___HP400	*Susannah's Secret*, K. Comeaux	___HP483	*Forever Is Not Long Enough*,
___HP403	*The Best Laid Plans*, C. M. Parker		B. Youree
___HP407	*Sleigh Bells*, J. M. Miller	___HP484	*The Heart Knows*, E. Bonner
___HP408	*Destinations*, T. H. Murray	___HP488	*Sonoran Sweetheart*, N. J. Farrier
___HP411	*Spirit of the Eagle*, G. Fields	___HP491	*An Unexpected Surprise*, R. Dow
___HP412	*To See His Way*, K. Paul	___HP492	*The Other Brother*, L. N. Dooley
___HP415	*Sonoran Sunrise*, N. J. Farrier	___HP495	*With Healing in His Wings*,
___HP416	*Both Sides of the Easel*, B. Youree		S. Krueger
___HP419	*Captive Heart*, D. Mindrup	___HP496	*Meet Me with a Promise*, J. A. Grote
___HP420	*In the Secret Place*, P. Griffin	___HP499	*Her Name Was Rebekah*,
___HP423	*Remnant of Forgiveness*, S. Laity		B. K. Graham
___HP424	*Darling Cassidy*, T. V. Bateman	___HP500	*Great Southland Gold*, M. Hawkins
___HP427	*Remnant of Grace*, S. K. Downs	___HP503	*Sonoran Secret*, N. J. Farrier
___HP428	*An Unmasked Heart*, A. Boeshaar	___HP504	*Mail-Order Husband*, D. Mills
___HP431	*Myles from Anywhere*, J. Stengl	___HP507	*Trunk of Surprises*, D. Hunt
___HP432	*Tears in a Bottle*, G. Fields	___HP508	*Dark Side of the Sun*, R. Druten
___HP435	*Circle of Vengeance*, M. J. Conner	___HP511	*To Walk in Sunshine*, S. Laity
___HP436	*Marty's Ride*, M. Davis	___HP512	*Precious Burdens*, C. M. Hake
___HP439	*One With the Wind*, K. Stevens	___HP515	*Love Almost Lost*, I. B. Brand
___HP440	*The Stranger's Kiss*, Y. Lehman	___HP516	*Lucy's Quilt*, J. Livingston
___HP443	*Lizzy's Hope*, L. A. Coleman	___HP519	*Red River Bride*, C. Coble
___HP444	*The Prodigal's Welcome*, K. Billerbeck	___HP520	*The Flame Within*, P. Griffin
___HP447	*Viking Pride*, D. Mindrup	___HP523	*Raining Fire*, L. A. Coleman
___HP448	*Chastity's Angel*, L. Ford	___HP524	*Laney's Kiss*, T. V. Bateman
___HP451	*Southern Treasures*, L. A. Coleman	___HP531	*Lizzie*, L. Ford
___HP452	*Season of Hope*, C. Cox	___HP532	*A Promise Made*, J. L. Barton
___HP455	*My Beloved Waits*, P. Darty	___HP535	*Viking Honor*, D. Mindrup
___HP456	*The Cattle Baron's Bride*, C. Coble	___HP536	*Emily's Place*, T. V. Bateman
___HP459	*Remnant of Light*, T. James	___HP539	*Two Hearts Wait*, F. Chrisman

(If ordering from this page, please remember to include it with the order form.)

Presents

Great Inspirational Romance at a Great Price!

Heartsong Presents books are inspirational romances in contemporary and historical settings, designed to give you an enjoyable, spirit-lifting reading experience. You can choose wonderfully written titles from some of today's best authors like Peggy Darty, Sally Laity, DiAnn Mills, Colleen L. Reece, Debra White Smith, and many others.

When ordering quantities less than twelve, above titles are $2.97 each.
Not all titles may be available at time of order.